TWO ACTION-PACKED
ENDWORLD ADVENTURES
IN ONE LOW-PRICED VOLUME!

ATLANTA RUN

Hickory took a step, his eyes on the aircraft. "Look! It's diving."

Blade tensed as the plane banked and dove. "Move it!"

The gunfighter ignored the command, his hands flashing to his pearl-handled Magnums. A pattern of exploding turf stitched a direct pattern toward Hickok, who calmly stood firm and blasted from the hip.

The gunner in the plane was concentrating on Hickok. His shots came within inches of the gunfighter's moccasins as the craft winged within 20 feet of the Warrior's head....

MEMPHIS RUN

Three of the squad were still standing. A man with a scar on his chin raised his M-16 to shoot, but took a slug in his right eye that spun him completely around and stopped him in his tracks.

Only two left. Both were within six feet of Blade, one to his left, the other his right. With consummate skill, Blade raised the knives overhead and threw. The blades glistened in the sunlight as they flew into the chests of their respective targets. Twelve inches of cold steel were imbedded to the hilt in each Hound. Both men looked astonished; both dropped their machine guns and clutched at the Bowies; both gawked at Blade in amazement for a moment; and both sank into eternity without uttering a sound.

D1714969

The *Endworld Double* Series:

CAPITAL RUN/NEW YORK RUN
LIBERTY RUN/HOUSTON RUN
ANAHEIM RUN/SEATTLE RUN
NEVADA RUN/MIAMI RUN

ATLANTA RUN/ MEMPHIS RUN
DAVID ROBBINS

LEISURE BOOKS   NEW YORK CITY

Dedicated to my beloved family—
Judy,
Joshua,
and Shane.
As the song says:
"You are my everything...."

A LEISURE BOOK®

July 1992

Published by

Dorchester Publishing Co., Inc.
276 Fifth Avenue
New York, NY 10001

ATLANTA RUN

Prologue

The woman paused on the crest of the low hill and glanced over her right shoulder at the twinkling lights of the metropolis a mile distant. The wind whipped her brown hair into her green eyes, and she swiped at the lashing strands with her left hand. Held in her right arm, clutched close to her breast, was her child.

There was no sign of pursuit; the highway behind them was deserted.

Good.

Their escape had gone unnoticed.

She smiled in triumph as she faced to the south and fled into the night. The prospect of bumping into a mutant chilled her blood, but there wasn't any other choice. If she stopped, if she sought shelter from the elements, she risked being discovered by a Terminator patrol. The Terminators frequently ranged more than a mile from Atlanta, so she wasn't in the clear yet.

Another mile should do it.

"Mommy?"

"Not now, Chastity."

"I'm scared."

"There's nothing to be scared of."

"You're scared, Mommy."

The woman looked at the upturned, cherubic features of her six-year-old, barely visible in the gloom, and wrapped her left arm around Chastity's back for added support. "Why do you say that?"

"I can feel it," Chastity replied.

Annoyed by her failure to conceal her fright, the woman faked a broad smile. "You're imaginging things, dearest. I'm fine. Just a little cold, is all."

"So am I," Chastity said, tightening the grip of her thin arms about her mother's neck.

The woman breathed deeply as she jogged down the hill. She could feel her daughter's legs encircling her narrow waist, could feel the tension in those legs, and her conscience was pricked by guilt. Was freedom worth endangering Chastity's life? Was it that precious?

How could she ask such a stupid question?

"Mommy?"

"Please, Chastity. Not now. We must keep quiet."

"But the Bubbleheads are coming."

Startled, the woman halted and spun. Her gaze fixed on the top of the hill as a lightning flash far to the north silhouetted its sloping contours.

And there they were! Four Terminators, outlined against the sky! But how? Where had they come from?

"Mommy?" Chastity asked fearfully.

Struggling to suppress a rising sense of panic, the woman bolted southward. What should she do? Take cover in the woods? The Terminators would find them easily! But fleeing was even more foolish; she couldn't hope to outrun a Terminator Squad.

"The Bubbleheads are coming," Chastity reiterated.

"Quiet!" the mother ordered, angling to the right, leaving the highway and darting into the underbrush. She crashed through a thicket, turning her body sideways so her right side absorbed the brunt of their passage, her right shoulder and naked forearms slashed by the sharp branches.

Another streak of lightning, much nearer this time, served to briefly illuminate a small clearing and the wall of trees beyond. Seconds later, thunder boomed.

The woman plunged into the forest, weaving among the trunks, dreading a misstep. She was grateful for the steadily strenghtening wind; the rustling leaves and the crackling limbs would cover the sounds of her flight. But the Terminators would rely on more than hearing to track her down; they would use their Heat Vision.

Their damn, infallible Heat Vision!

She winced as her left foot sank in a rut and she twisted her ankle, and she nearly toppled forward. With a grunt, she righted herself and raced to the west. Her left ankle was throbbing, but she ignored the discomfort, endeavoring to maintain a clear head, to formulate a plan for eluding the Terminators, undaunted by a sobering realization: No one ever eluded the Terminators.

A raindrop spattered her face.

The mother paused, elation washing over her. There was a chance, after all! Not much of one, true, but one nonetheless. If only the rain would increase!

More rain descended, the drops heavy and cold, smacking the turf and the vegetation in an irregular rhythm.

She continued deeper into the woods, frantically seeking a hiding place, scrutinizing the inky vegetation, availing herself of the periodic lightning flashes to note landmarks, to get her bearings. During one such flash a huge tree materialized 20 yards ahead, its overhanging limbs forming a spreading canopy. The tree was perched halfway up a partially eroded knoll. Several enormous roots were exposed, two of which crisscrossed one another after looping outward and upward, then disappeared in the dank earth.

The rain became a steady drizzle, ever building.

The mother dashed toward the tree, squinting as the raindrops pelted her face, her eyes. She reached the base of the knoll and hurriedly inspected the root system, and grinned at the discovery of a two-foot space between the crisscrossed roots and the slope.

"Mommy," Chastity said softly.

"Quiet," the mother chided. She squatted and slid behind the roots, her back to the knoll, her blue jumpsuit clammy on her skin.

"What will the Bubbleheads do?" Chastity asked.

"Be quiet!" the woman repeated.

With a rush of wind and an abrupt deluge of rain, the summer storm attained its peak of primal fury. The nearby trees bowed their crowns to Nature's majesty, and the driving sheets of precipitation obscured the landscape.

The mother was overjoyed, knowing the storm would hamper the Terminators. If the tempest persisted long enough, the Terminator Squad might call off the hunt.

"I have to tinkle," Chastity said in her mom's left ear.

"Not now."

"I have to go," Chastity insisted.

"Do you want the Bubbleheads to find us?" the mother demanded.

"No."

"Then keep quiet! And hold it in until we're sure the Bubbleheads are gone."

"Yes, Mommy," Chastity said, and sighed.

The woman peered out, leaning to the left, water cascading over her head and shoulders. She blinked her eyes to clear her vision, striving to detect movement in the undergrowth.

Where the hell were the Terminators?

Had the squad given up already?

No.

She spotted a silvery shape to the left, perhaps 15 yards off, and the shape was moving! The form was advancing slowly toward the knoll. She ducked from sight and pressed her forehead against the roots, clasping Chastity to her bosom. "Shhhh!" she whispered. "Don't make a sound."

For once, her daughter obeyed.

The rain was drumming on the ground and thumping on the uncovered side of the root system. Combined with the swishing of the wind, the shaking of the trees, and the intermittent crack of thunder, the storm was creating a constant racket, the din effectively deadening the tread of the Terminator's silver boots.

Where *was* the Terminator?

Her curiosity getting the better of her, the mother eased

her head to the left and risked a hasty peek. And froze, terrified.

The Terminator was five feet from the roots, his back to the knoll, the silver dome of his head sweeping from right to left and back again. The three slim, silver tanks between his shoulder blades were visible. His silver left hand, the fingers splayed, was on his left hip. In his right hand, which was draped at his side, was the Fryer nozzle.

She gaped at the Fryer, recalling the time she had seen a Disruptive slain by a Terminator Squad. The stench of the poor man's burning flesh had sickened her.

Chastity shifted uncomfortably.

The mother placed her lips next to her daughter's right ear. "Shhh," she warned in a scarcely audible voice.

The Terminator started to turn.

Startled, the mother ducked from sight. Had he spotted her? She held her breath, her frightened eyes glued to the open space to the left of the roots, waiting for the Terminator to appear. A minute elapsed. She resumed breathing.

The storm was still in full swing.

With extreme caution, she inched to the left and peeped out.

He was gone!

She grinned as she craned her neck for a better look, astonished at her good fortune. The rumor she'd heard must be true. Rain *did* interfere with their Heat Vision! Otherwise, the Terminator would have detected Chastity and her. She leaned back and patted Chastity's head. "It's all right, honey. The Bubbleheads won't get us."

"Can I go to the bathroom now?"

"In a bit."

"I have to go bad, Mommy."

"All right. Let me make sure the coast is clear, and then you can go."

"Okay."

The mother shifted and deposited Chastity on the ground at the base of the crisscrossed roots. "You're to stay put.

Do you understand?''

Chastity nodded.

"I don't want you to move a muscle until I get back,'' the mother reiterated.

"I won't, Mommy,'' Chastity promised.

"Good.'' The mother moved to the left and paused in the opening. "Remember,'' she cautioned in a whisper, "don't budge until I come back.''

"Why can't I go right here?'' Chastity inquired.

"We might need to stay here for a while,'' the mother responded. "Just stay where you are. I'll be right back.''

"Okay,'' Chastity said, and sighed.

The mother stepped into the rain, the drops pummeling her head and shoulders, the water splattering her eyes. She pressed her right hand, palm down, to her forehead and surveyed the immediate vicinity. A lightning strike to the east lit up the heavens, casting the forest in stark relief. She could see the tree limbs whipping in the wind, and the bushes quaking, the weeds shaking, but there was no sign of the Terminator. Emboldened, she walked toward the nearest trees, constantly scanning in all directions. When she was 15 yards from the knoll she halted, grinning.

They had done it!

Now all they had to do was wait out the storm!

She turned, her happy expression transforming into a horrified countenance, her left arm extending in a defensive gesture. "No!'' she blurted out.

"Yes!'' responded the Terminator, standing not four feet from her, his voice muffled by his headpiece. He held the Fryer nozzle at waist height.

She glanced over his right shoulder at the knoll, hoping Chastity was staying hidden.

"Did you really think you'd get away with it?'' the Terminator demanded, talking loudly to be heard above the downpour.

"I had to try.''

"You're a fool!'' the Terminator declared.

The mother said nothing.

"Where is the child?'' he asked.

"What child?"

"Don't play games with me," the Terminator stated testily.

"I don't know what you're talking about."

The Terminator swiveled the Fryer nozzle, pointing the tip at her. "Make this easy on yourself. Tell me where the child is."

The mother's lips compressed into a thin line, signifying her defiance.

"We'll find her," the Terminator said. "It's only a matter of time."

She refused to speak.

"Wouldn't you prefer to go out together?" he queried. "It would be better for her."

"As if you had her best interest at heart!" the woman snapped. "Don't make me laugh!"

"And you do?" the Terminator retorted. "You're kidding no one but yourself, lady. If you really cared for the kid, you wouldn't have pulled this stupid stunt."

"How did you find out?" she asked.

"How do you think?" he replied.

"One of the monitors picked us up?" she asked.

The Terminator shook his head. "Guess again."

"My apartment was bugged."

He laughed, a hollow sound under his headpiece. "You flatter yourself. You weren't even under surveillance."

"Then how . . ." she began, then stopped, insight flooding her mind. "No!"

"Yes," the Terminator responded. "How else?"

"An Informer!"

"Of course," he confirmed.

"But that's impossible!" the mother exclaimed. "I only told one person."

"One too many," he said.

"No!" she declared. "I refuse to believe you! I told the one person I trust completely."

"Misplaced trust," he commented.

"You're lying," she stubbornly persisted.

"Am I?" the Terminator replied. "Then how did we

know which road you would be taking? How did we know tonight was the night?'' He paused. ''Ten thousand dollars is a lot of money.''

The realization that he was telling the truth hit her harder than any physical blow possibly could, and she took a step backwards, shaking her head, emotionally staggered. ''You're just saying that!''

''You know better.''

She stared skyward, an upwelling of tears commingling with the raindrops.

''Now where is your daughter?'' the Terminator probed.

Her face, upturned to the clouds and the storm, was inexpressibly sad.

''Where the hell is your daughter?''

She did not respond.

The Terminator shrugged. ''Suit yourself.''

The mother looked at him. ''May God have mercy on your soul.''

''God?'' The Terminator chuckled. ''You *are* way off the deep end, aren't you? There is no God. The Civil Council made that determination decades ago.''

''And you believe them?''

''What a dumb-ass question!'' he retorted. ''The Civil Council wouldn't mislead us.''

''The Civil Council is a pack of lying degenerates,'' she said bitterly.

''We can add treason to your list of crimes,'' the Terminator remarked. ''Anything else?''

''There is a God.''

He shook his head. ''Pitiful! You're insane, lady! You know the saying. Divinity is depravity; humanity is reality.''

''I was taught the same garbage in school.''

The Terminator hefted the Fryer. ''I've listened to enough of your sedition, to your blasphemy against the Council.''

''Don't I get a last request?'' she asked.

''No,'' the Terminator said, then squeezed the trigger on the nuzzle. The flames engulfed the woman before she could hope to react, the intensity of the heat only slightly reduced by the dampening effect of the rain. She staggered backwards, waving her arms, screaming in torment as her blue cotton jump suit combusted and her skin fried. He took a stride closer, sweeping the nozzle up and down, directing the blistering flames from her head to her feet. Her hair was on fire. He watched her fall to her knees, her movements becoming weaker and weaker, and he poured on the flames, relishing the sight of her charred features, of her gaping, blackened lips. She pitched onto her face, her body ablaze, convulsing for several moments before lying still. He let up on the Fryer and stared at her smoldering corpse as the rain quickly extinguished his handiwork. ''Stupid bitch,'' he muttered, and pivoted, scrutinizing the trees.

Now where was the brat?

Chapter One

"I'm tired of all this blamed walkin'," remarked the blond man in buckskins.

"Quit your griping," said the giant.

"I'm not gripin'," the man in buckskins responded. "I'm simply makin' a point."

"Which is?" the giant asked.

"That we should find a buggy somewhere and borrow it," suggested the one in buckskins. His long blond hair complemented his sweeping moustache of the same color. Around his waist were strapped a pair of Colt Python revolvers, and over his left shoulder was slung an Uzi.

The third member of their party, a small, wiry man dressed all in black, glanced at the man in buckskins. "Borrow it? You mean steal it."

"Call it what you want, Rikki," the blond man said. "we need a vehicle. At the rate we're going, we won't reach the Home for a year."

The one in black nodded. His hair and eyes were both dark. An Uzi was over his right shoulder, and slanted under his black belt, aligned over his left hip, was a long, black scabbard containing his prized katana. "I agree we need a vehicle. But do we have the right to steal one?"

"Out here," the blond man commented, patting his Pythons, "might makes right."

Rikki's eyes narrowed. "You would take a vehicle at gunpoint, Hickok?"

"If need be," Hickok replied.

"Warriors should not stoop to stealing," Rikki commented.

"We can't afford to be finicky," Hickok said. "Do you want to see your girlfriend before she becomes an old maid?"

"I miss Lexine," Rikki admitted.

"And I can't wait to see my missus and young'un again," Hickok declared. "The sooner, the better. Which means we must find a car or truck."

The man in black glanced at the giant. "What do you say, Blade? Who's right?"

The seven-foot-tall powerhouse looked from Rikki to Hickok. "You both are."

Hickok squinted up at the Herculean figure in the black leather vest, fatigue pants, and combat boots. "Are you loco? How can we both be right?"

Blade idly placed his hands on the hilts of his Bowies, each big knife snug in its sheath, one on each hip. An M-16 was draped over his broad left shoulder. "You're right," he told the gunman, "because we do need transportation."

Hickok smirked and gazed at Rikki. "See?"

"But Rikki has a valid point," Blade went on. "We can't steal a car or truck from the first person we bump into who owns one."

"I didn't know there are rules of etiquette for swipin' a buggy," Hickok stated sarcastically.

Blade sighed and stared up at the bright blue sky, feeling the heat of the July sun on his rugged features, his gray eyes troubled. He ran his right hand through his dark hair. "We need a vehicle," he reiterated. "There's no denying that. We're stranded, and we're approximately fifteen hundred miles from Minnesota."

"It's not our fault the blasted Hurricane never came back to pick us up," Hickok muttered.

Blade frowned as he scrutinized the terrain ahead, a flat stretch of lushly forested landscape. The gunman had hit the proverbial nail on the head: their predicament was not their fault. Recent events swept through his mind in a rush, and he remembered all of the factors involved in their dilemma.

First, there was the Home, the survivalist compound situated in northern Minnesota where they had been born and raised. Constructed by a wealthy idealist prior to World War Three, the Home was occupied by the Founder's descendants, dubbed the Family. And as three of the Warrior class, those responsible for defending the Home and protecting the Family, Blade, Rikki, and Hickok were pledged to eliminate any threat.

Enter the Dragons. Until a couple of weeks ago, the Dragons had ruled southern Florida like medieval masters over a serfdom. Florida had not fared well during the war. The state had devolved into anarchy after the collapse of the federal and state governments, and into the vacuum came the drug lords, rival gangs fighting to control. One drug organization eventually triumphed: the Dragons. But they made the mistake of plotting the Family's downfall, and now, thanks to the three Warriors, the leaders of the Dragons were dead and their drug empire was in disarray.

So the Warriors had accomplished their mission.

Which was all well and good.

Unfortunately, they had found themselves left high and dry, inexplicably abandoned. The Hurricane, the jet with VTOL capability that had conveyed them from Minnesota to Florida, never showed up at the rendezvous site, never retrieved them as scheduled.

Which meant they were compelled to walk back, through a land overrun with mutants, mutates, scavengers, and sundry menaces of every description.

Why? Blade asked himself.

Why didn't the Hurricane show up? Had it crashed? Had something else happened to the craft?

Or *worse*.

Had something happened to the Freedom Federation?

The Federation was the brainchild of the leaders of the seven factions constituting its membership. Where once fifty states had been united to preserve the national identity of the United States, now seven scattered factions were devoted to maintaining the flickering light of civilization and wresting humankind from the darkness of savage barbarism. The Family was but one of the seven. Also included were the Moles and the Clan, both groups located in Minnesota. The fourth faction controlled the Dakota Territory; they were a group of superb horsemen known as the Cavalry. The Flathead Indians in Montana had also joined the Federation, as had the Civilized Zone, a large area in the Midwest.

And finally, the latest addition to the Freedom Federation was the Free State of California. Unlike Florida, California had been one of the few states to retain its administrative integrity after the war. California had consolidated its National Guard, and all of the Army, Navy, Air Force, and Marine units within its borders, into a cohesive force, enabling the state to withstand the hordes of looters and the chaos resulting from the unleashing of the nuclear holocaust. California's leaders had wisely opted to diligently maintain their technological capabilities, and as part of that goal they placed special emphasis on the importance of their Air Force, particularly their Hurricanes. As a gesture of goodwill, the governor of California had offered to employ the Hurricanes in a regular shuttle and messenger service between the Federation members.

Blade had commandeered one of the Hurricanes, prevailing upon the pilot to fly Hickok, Rikki, and himself to Florida. As he reviewed the sequence of events, he found himself regretting that action. Here they were, cut off, abandoned, hundreds and hundreds of miles from their loved ones. Perhaps he should have . . .

". . . listenin' to me or what?" Hickok demanded.

The giant abruptly realized he'd been completely distracted by his thoughts. "Sorry," he said. "What did you say?"

"What's the matter with you, pard?" Hickok inquired. "Did that fracas with the Dragons addle your brain?"

Blade smiled. "No. What were you saying?"

"I want to know how we're going to get our hands on a car or truck," Hickok mentioned. "I doubt anybody will just give us one."

Rikki suddenly stopped and held his right hand aloft for silence. "I hear an engine," he told them.

Blade cocked his head to one side, listening. For a moment he heard only the insects and the birds, but then, from off to the southeast, arose a sustained growl.

"It's a plane!" Hickok declared, scanning the heavens.

"There," Rikki said, pointing.

Blade spotted it too. A small, white, single-engine aircraft approaching at a steady clip.

"I wish I had my Henry," Hickok remarked, referring to his favorite rifle, a weapon he'd lost in Florida. "I'd try and shoot it down."

"Why?" Rikki asked. "What good would shooting it down do?"

"The pilot might know where we could find a vehicle," the gunman replied.

"Provided he survived the crash," Rikki noted.

"Nitpick, nitpick," Hickok grumbled.

Blade smiled as he studied the plane, speculating on its destination. The aircraft was bearing to the northwest. He extracted a map from his left rear pocket and unfolded it.

"Where do you figure we are?" Hickok queried.

"In Georgia," Blade said, crouching and placing the map on the ground. "Or what was once Georgia." They'd deliberately avoided every inhabited settlement, knowing from prior experience that the likelihood of receiving a friendly reception was slim. According to the Family Elders—and substantiated by the thousands of volumes in the library the Founder had personally stocked at the Home—social customs had been drastically different before the war. One hundred and five years ago a person could travel from town to town, from city to city, without having to fear for his or her life. But nowadays, people were inclined to shoot first and ascertain peaceful intent later— if a stranger survived long enough to be able to convince them. To preclude such an eventuality, the Warriors had bypassed towns and communities betraying evidence of habitation, and because they were sticking to the less-traveled byways and proceeding overland where possible, Blade could not pinpoint their exact location with precise accuracy. "I think we're about twenty miles southeast of Atlanta. If Atlanta is still there."

"Do you reckon it was nuked?" Hickok asked.

"I don't know," Blade responded.

"The plane," Rikki said.

"What about it?" Blade inquired, looking up.

"It's coming toward us," the man in black said.

Blade stood, the map in his right hand, surprised to see the plane deviating slightly from its course, slanting in their direction.

"Maybe the pilot has seen us," Hickok suggested.

Blade glanced around. They were standing in the middle of a field, 40 yards from the trees. He gazed at the small plane again, wondering if the craft was outfitted with armaments.

"I don't like this," Rikki stated.

The plane was less than a thousand feet above the ground and several hundred yards distant.

Blade looked at the Family's supreme martial artist. Rikki-Tikki-Tavi's intuition was rarely wrong; if he sensed danger, then there was danger. "Head for the woods."

Hickok took a step, his eyes on the aircraft. "Look! It's diving!"

Blade tensed as the plane banked and dove. "Move it!" he shouted, and suited action to words by sprinting for the forest, automatically running a zigzag pattern to minimize the target he posed.

Hickok and Rikki followed suit, separating.

Blade could hear the roar of the engine as the aircraft swooped toward them. He glanced over his left shoulder, seeing the plane level off and someone stick a gun barrel out a window on the passenger side. "Down!" he yelled, and threw himself to the earth, bruising his left forearm on a rock.

There was the brittle barking of a machine gun from overhead. The grass and weeds near the giant erupted in miniature geysers as heavy slugs plowed into the ground.

Blade rolled to the right and leaped to his feet as the craft climbed for another strafing attack. He saw Hickok and Rikki already in motion, and he raced after them. Would the plane have time for another try before they reached the shelter of the forest?

Yes.

The three Warriors were 20 yards from cover when the aircraft completed executing a tight loop and dove again.

Hickok abruptly halted and spun.

The plane's engine was whining.

Blade slowed, gazing at the gunman ten yards to his left. "Run!" he ordered.

The gunfighter ignored the command, his hands flashing to his pearl-handled Magnums, the Colts clearing leather at the same instant the gunner in the aircraft opened fire. A pattern of exploding turf stitched a direct path toward Hickok, who calmly stood firm and blasted from the hip.

Frowning in annoyance, Blade quickly brought the M-16 into play, stopping and raising the automatic rifle to his right shoulder and squeezing off a hurried burst.

Rikki-Tikki-Tavi joined in with his Uzi.

The gunner in the plane was concentrating on Hickok. His shots came within inches of the gunfighter's moccasins as the craft winged within 20 feet of the Warrior's head.

Hickok never flinched. He methodically fired his Pythons, pacing his shots one after the other, standing rooted to the spot as the earth sprayed over his feet and legs. As the plane passed overhead he turned, tracking it, his Colts booming in a regular cadence.

The plane started to climb when there was a loud coughing noise and black smoke billowed from underneath its fuselage.

All three Warriors ceased firing.

Belching more smoke, its engine sputtering, the aircraft slowly climbed to the northwest, the sun glinting off its wings.

"Serves them varmints right," Hickok declared.

Blade walked over to the gunman. "What were you trying to prove? You could have gotten yourself killed."

Hickock was watching the departing plane. "That cow chip was a lousy shot. I counted on him to miss."

"You deliberately drew their fire?"

"He did," Rikki said, coming up to them. "He knew we could not reach the trees. He was trying to save us."

Blade shook his head in disapproval. "That was a stupid stunt. There was no need to sacrifice yourself for us. We're perfectly capable of taking care of ourselves."

Hickok began ejecting the spent cartridges from his Pythons. "I promised your missus I'd make sure you got back in one piece."

"I don't need a baby-sitter," Blade said angrily.

Hickok glanced at Rikki and winked. "Every man needs a baby-sitter, pard. Why do you think we get hitched?"

Chapter Two

"We'll be taking a risk," Rikki commented.

"I know," Blade responded. "But we're all thirsty, and a few sips shouldn't hurt us. We can't afford to take the time to build a fire and boil the water."

"Besides which," Hickok noted, "we don't have anything to boil the water *in*."

The three Warriors were walking toward a narrow stream at the base of a hill located five miles from the field where the aircraft had attacked them.

Rikki stared at the slowly flowing water 12 yards away. "The stream could be contaminated," he stressed.

Blade knew the martial artist was making a valid point. The environment was severely polluted, thanks to all of the radioactive and chemical toxins tainting the biological chain. Streams, creeks, and ponds often appeared to be pure and harmless, but a single swallow could result in a lingering, painful death. He gazed at the water ahead, debating the wisdom of allowing them to drink.

A small fish unexpectedly leaped out of the stream and splashed down again, apparently going for a hovering insect.

Blade relaxed. If there were fish present in any body of water, invariably the water was safe to consume, if in limited quantities.

"I wish we hadn't lost our gear in Florida," Hickok

groused. "A canteen would come in handy right about now."

"You know," Blade said to the gunman, "you're turning into a real grump."

Hickok was opening his mouth to reply, a stinging retort on his lips, when a high-pitched scream sounded from the dense forest on the far side of the stream.

Rikki-Tikki-Tavi was off before the scream died down, racing to the near edge of the water and vaulting into the air, clearing the four-foot stream effortlessly. He landed on the balls of his feet, then dashed into the undergrowth.

"Rikki!" Blade shouted, jogging forward. "Wait for us!"

But the martial artist wasn't about to slacken his pace. His keen hearing had registered a terrified, wavering quality to the shriek, and something else as well: the unmistakable vocal traits of a child. He darted around a tree and skirted a bush, looking to the right and the left.

A second screech rent the muggy air, coming from the left.

Rikki dashed in the direction of the cry, disregarding the limbs tearing at his clothes and impeding his progress. The trees abruptly thinned. Five seconds later he reached a circular clearing and drew up short, his right hand gripping the hilt of his katana, his eyes widening in consternation.

He had found the child.

She was a girl of five or so, attired in a filthy blue jumpsuit and brown shoes, her shoulder-length blonde hair soiled and plastered to her head. As she perched on top of a large log bisecting the center of the clearing, her gaze was riveted on the creature glaring up at her.

A huge wild boar stood next to the log, its upturned yellowish tusks mere inches from the girl's trembling legs. Four feet at the shoulder, six feet in length, and weighing over 380 pounds, the boar was a hideous sight with its seven-inch tusks, long, bristly hair, pronounced snout, and beady, feral eyes. It grunted and lunged at the girl.

She tottered backwards, her arms waving wildly, her face

a mask of fear.

Rikki realized the girl was on the verge of falling. He whipped the katana from its scabbard, taking hold of the hilt in both hands, and assumed a squatting stance with the sword upraised. "Ho! Boar!" he yelled. "Try me!"

The wild boar whirled at the Warrior's challenge, uttering a raspy squeal and lowering its head defensively.

The girl was frozen on the log, gawking at the man in black in astonishment.

"Try me!" Rikki repeated.

As if accepting the challenge, the boar charged, its hooves digging into the turf and sending dirt flying. Like a four-legged tank, and with startling speed, the boar barreled toward the audacious interloper.

Rikki-Tikki-Tavi seemed to be carved from marble. Not a muscle twitched until the onrushing juggernaut was within a yard of his coiled form, and then he struck with the un-surpassed swiftness of a perfected swordsmaster. His body was a blur as he sidestepped and arced the katana down. The razor edge sliced into the boar's neck.

Unable to check its assault, the boar was six yards past its foe before it could turn. Blood spurted from its slit neck, but the fierce swine was oblivious to the wound. A single-minded purpose dominated its bestial heart; the boar wanted to rend and tear the human in black.

His bloody katana uplifted, Rikki awaited the second charge. An insidious thought crept into his mind as he watched the boar shake its head and bellow: What were the odds of evading those tusks again? Annoyed at his lack of concentration, Rikki emptied himself of all contem-plation. To be one with the sword, to perform flawlessly, he must suppress all conscious deliberation, must react instinctively. The sword had to become an extension of his arms, as much a part of him as his limbs.

The wild boar came on once more.

Rikki crouched, an empty vessel devoid of will, functioning on the reflexive level of conditioned response. The countless hours he'd spent in practicing his technique, in honing his skills, were about to reap a crucial reward: his life.

The nasty tusks slashed at the Warrior's midriff as the boar closed.

The martial artist took a quick stride to the left, tucking in his abdomen to avoid the boar's blow and countering with a glittering swipe of his sword. The katana cut into the creature's head above its enraged eyes, cleaving the flesh and penetrating the bone underneath before Rikki wrenched the blade free.

Crimson poured down the boar's face as it rotated for a third attempt.

Rikki risked a glance to see if the girl was still on the log. She was gone!

The wild boar pounded toward its adversary, lowering its head to slash with its tusks.

Rikki leaped, his compact, steely muscles carrying him above the hurtling swine. At the apex of his jump he was directly over the boar's head, and he reversed his grip on the katana, grasping the hilt with the sword vertical, the point angled straight down. Gravity combined with his momentum to do the rest. The tip of the blade speared into the boar's cranium between its hairy, triangular ears, lancing several inches into the creature's skull. Rikki held on tight, his feet suspended inches above the ground, as the boar bucked and heaved.

The animal abruptly sprawled forward onto its front knees, wheezing and sputtering.

Rikki braced his legs on the turf and jerked the katana loose. He turned and surveyed the log and the trees beyond, perplexed. Where could the girl have gone? Why would she leave?

A throaty grunt intruded on his musing from the right.

The martial artist twirled, starting to raise the katana, knowing he'd been careless, that there must be a second boar.

There was.

Already charging the man in black, the other swine was

smaller than the first, but still endowed with five-inch tusks and weighing nearly 300 pounds. Less than six feet separated it from the human.

Rikki perceived his danger in a fraction of a second. The boar would be on him before he could shift position.

The booming of gunfire rocked the clearing, and the boar's thick hide was perforated again and again by a hail of slugs from an M-16 and an Uzi. The impact staggered the creature, causing the swine to stumble to one side, its rush arrested by the lead tearing through its squat form. In torment, confused and ignorant of the source of its pain, it faced in the direction of the thundering guns. More rounds smacked into its head, puncturing its eyes, forehead, and snout. The boar squealed once, then dropped.

"Anyone for a barbecue?"

Rikki turned.

Blade and Hickok were at the edge of the clearing, their automatic weapons cradled in their hands.

"Piece of cake," Hickok quipped, strolling over to the boar they'd shot. "Where's the third one?"

"The third one?" Rikki repeated, puzzled.

"Sure," Hickok said with a grin. "Haven't you ever read *The Three Little Pigs*?"

Blade advanced, scrutinizing the trees enclosing them. "Who was screaming?"

Rikki glanced at the log. "A small girl with blonde hair."

"Where is she?" Blade asked.

"She disappeared," Rikki said.

"Maybe it was Goldilocks," Hickok suggested, chuckling.

Rikki walked to the log, his forehead creased, trying to imagine the girl's reason for fleeing. He stared at the top of the log, then leaned over to check the other side.

And there she was, on her hands and knees, her smudged face tilted upwards, her frightened blue eyes on the Warrior.

"Hello," Rikki said softly, smiling reassuringly.

The girl didn't budge.

"I am Rikki-Tikki-Tavi," the martial artist introduced himself. "Who are you?"

Blade and Hickok came over, Blade on Rikki's left, the gunman to the right.

Whining in terror, the girl rose to her knees, about to run.

"Don't!" Rikki said. "We are friends!"

She hesitated, looking from one to the other.

"Howdy there, little lady," Hickok declared, beaming. "What are you doing in his neck of the woods? Lookin' for Little Red Riding Hood's house?"

The girl shook her head.

"Then you must be lookin' for the Three Bears," the gunman said. "But I don't think they're home right now. They're out collectin' honey."

Again the girl shook her head.

Hickok sighed and leaned his right arm on the top of the log. "I give up. What the dickens are you doing out here?"

"Hiding," she answered, her voice a tremulous whisper.

"Hiding?" Hickok said, glancing around. "Who's after you? The Big, Bad Wolf? I'll blow the critter away!"

"The Bubbleheads," the girl disclosed.

Hickok did a double take. "I don't believe I know them varmints. But I won't let them hurt you."

"Promise?"

"I promise," the gunman pledged. He extended his right hand. "I'm pleased to meet you. My handle is Hickok."

"Handle?"

"Sorry. My name is Hickok."

The girl studied the gunfighter for a moment, then reached up and took his hand. "You're a good man," she said simply.

Hickok smiled as he shook. "You should tell that to my missus. Sometimes she has her doubts."

"What's a missus?"

"A missus is a wife," Hickok explained. "I have a wife named Sherry and a tadpole named Ringo."

The girl managed a weary grin. "Do you like frogs?"

"Frogs?"

"My mommy told me all about tadpoles," she mentioned. "They become frogs."

Blade laughed.

Hickok shook his head. "Not that kind of tadpole," he detailed. "I was talkin' about my young'un. He's a sprout like you."

The child, her right hand still resting in the gunman's, looked down at herself. "I'm not a sprout. I'm a girl."

Blade suppressed an impulse to cackle. "You need an interpreter," he told the gunman.

Hickok gingerly lifted the girl onto the log. "Come on up here," he said. "We need to have a palaver."

The child glanced at Rikki. "He talks funny."

"You don't know the half of it," Rikki said.

Hickok released her hand and sat down next to her. "You mentioned your mommy. Where is she?"

The girl's chin sagged and her lips quivered.

"Did something happen to your mommy?" Hickok questioned.

She gulped and nodded.

"What?"

"The Bubbleheads hurt her."

Hickok exchanged a confounded expression with his companions. "Who are the Bubbleheads?"

"They're bad men."

Hickok gently placed his right hand around her slim shoulders. "Listen . . ." He paused, then began again. "What's your name, anyway?"

"Chastity," the girl replied. "Chastity Snow."

"Well, Chastity, I know it might hurt to talk about it, but I need to know what happened to your mommy," Hickok said. "What did the Bubbleheads do to her?"

Chastity averted her eyes and trembled.

"There, there," Hickok said, soothing her. "Everything is okay. We'll help you. You can trust us."

Chastity gazed at the gunfighter, tears in the corners of her eyes. "I like you," she declared huskily.

"And I like you," Hickok assured her. "But I really must know what happened to your mommy. Will you tell me?"

"They burned her," Chastity answered, her voice barely audible.

"The Bubbleheads set your mom on fire?" Hickok asked.

Chastity nodded.

"Can you take us to where this happened?"

"Maybe," Chastity responded. "It's far."

"When was the last time you ate?" Blade interjected.

"I don't remember."

"You must be hungry," Blade commented, staring at the dead boars.

Chastity nodded.

"Then we'll roast some boar meat," Blade proposed, "and take off after we've eaten."

"I'll gather wood for the fire," Rikki offered, and walked toawrd the trees rimming the clearing to the north.

Chastity watched the man in black enter the forest. "He'd better be careful," she said.

"Don't worry about Rikki," Hickok remarked. "No boar will get him."

"The icky thing might see him," Chastity said, gazing apprehensively at the nearby foliage.

"What icky thing?" Hickok asked.

"She must mean a mutant," Blade deduced.

"You saw this icky thing?" Hickok queried her.

Chastity nodded. "Yesterday."

"What did it look like?"

"It was big and black and had two heads," Chastity replied.

"Definitely a mutant," Hickok stated. "And we won't let any mutant harm you."

Chastity smiled at the gunman. "I'm not scared now."

"Good," Hickok said. "Besides, the icky thing must be long gone."

At that moment, in contradiction to the gunman's assertion, a tremendous roar rent the woods to the east.

Chapter Three

"The icky thing!" Chastity cried.

Hickok slid to the far side of the log, pulling the girl after him. He crouched and surveyed the forest.

Blade took several strides to the east, leveling the M-16. The roar had been close, too close. Whatever made it was probably watching him at that very second. His gray eyes narrowed as he tried to detect a hint of movement in the undergrowth. If the roar came from a creature answering Chastity's description, then, as Hickok had noted, the thing was undoubtedly a wild mutant.

And the giant despised the savage, proliferating monstrosities.

Perhaps the reason was because his father had been killed by a genetic deviate. Perhaps he loathed them simply because they were gross aberrations of nature, a vile testimony to humankind's tampering with forces better left untouched. Perhaps it was because he'd known so many people who'd been killed or maimed by the horrid beasts.

Whatever his justification, he waited for the creature to appear with a mixture of dread and anticipation. Dread owing to his abhorrence, anticipation because he eagerly wanted to blast one of the things to kingdom come. As he scanned the brush and the trees, he thought of the three different types of mutations he'd encountered.

First, there were those mutations produced by the massive

radiation unleashed during the war. Deformed offspring were a frequent occurrence, young born with extra limbs or misplaced features. Of the three types, this kind was the most numerous.

Second were the especially repulsive fiends created by the chemical-warfare weapons. Known as mutates to distinguish them from the radiation-formed deviates, these demented, pus-covered brutes were even more feared than the typical mutants.

Third, and smallest in numbers, were those mutations specifically developed by the genetic engineers. In the years prior to the war, genetic engineering had been all the rage with the scientific community. Hybrids were bred, curious combinations of humans and animals, both before and after the nuclear exchange. A trio of such beings currently resided at the Home, and the Warrior considered them as friends.

Mutations of every variety were a fact of life in the postwar era. Blade could hardly conceive of what it must have been like before World War Three. A world without mutants was an alien concept; to be able to take a stroll in the woods without having to worry about being attacked sounded like Utopia. For the umpteenth time, he recognized that the people living before the war had not realized how good they had it.

A branch snapped to the left.

Blade swiveled, catching a glimpse of a dark form moving between two trees. Something big, just like Chastity had said. His finger stroked the cool metal trigger. Would the thing try to circle around the clearing? Did it know one of them had gone to the north? What if it went after Rikki? The martial artist must have heard the roar. Surely Rikki would return. . . .

Another stupendous roar shattered the tranquil wilderness as the creature attacked, bursting from cover and bounding toward the giant.

Blade took in the mutant's black, leathery, hairless skin, its bulky body and four heavy legs, its pear-shaped head, crazed eyes, slavering mouth, and its tapered teeth and talons, all in the instant before he fired. The M-16 chattered and bucked, and he saw his rounds slam into the thing's face and neck.

The mutant stumbled and almost went down, only to recover and surge across the eight feet separating it from its intended prey.

Blade emptied the magazine, hearing Hickok providing covering fire with the Uzi, and then the mutant was upon him, its bearlike torso plowing into him and knocking him onto his back. The thing snapped at his neck, but missed, and the Warrior responded by pounding the creature's right eye with the stock of the M-16.

Snarling in fury, the mutant opened its mouth wide to bite the human's throat.

Damn! Blade was partially pinned, with his legs trapped under the beast. His huge arm muscles rippled as he tilted the M-16 and rammed the barrel into the mutant's mouth.

The deviate gagged and gurgled, then backed away, six inches of the automatic rifle lodged in its maw, shaking its head vigorously to dislodge the weapon.

His legs were clear! Blade heaved erect, drawing the Bowies. He dove, his arms coming up and around, the tips of the knives pointed inward. The mutant was still striving to extricate the M-16. Blade plunged both knives into the creature's eyes, burying them as far as they would go, and held fast.

With a bellow of agony, the mutation tried to pull backwards, crimson spurting from its ravaged sockets.

On his knees, gripping the Bowie hilts with all of his strength, his hand and wrists covered with flowing blood, Blade struggled to prevent the beast from tugging loose. He expected to be raked by the four-inch talons on the creature's forelegs, but the mutant was engrossed in freeing itself from the knives. It took three steps rearward, dragging the Warrior along, its shoulders bunched, its head snapping back and forth.

Blade felt his left hand begin to slip. He applied more

pressure to the right Bowie to compensate, and saw Hickok appear to his left. The gunman was holding the Pythons, and as he materalized he aimed both revolvers at the mutant's cranium. But his aid was unnecessary.

The mutant suddenly collapsed, sinking to the turf with a gasp of fetid breath and going limp.

Hickok, the Pythons cocked, paused. "Is the critter dead?"

Blade released the left Bowie and straightened, examining the mutant's form for telltale breathing. There wasn't any. "I think it is," he answered, feeling a drumming sensation in his ears.

The gunman glanced to the north. "Here comes Rikki."

Rikki-Tikki-Tavi emerged from the forest and crossed toward them. "Are you two all right?" he asked in concern.

"We're fine," Hickok responded. "Blade had to tend to an uninvited supper guest, is all."

Rikki gazed at the giant for a moment. "You look flushed. Are you okay?"

"An adrenaline surge," Blade explained, standing slowly. He leaned down and wrenched the Bowies out.

"Should I continue searching for wood?" Rikki asked.

"Yes," Blade replied. He started to wipe the knives clean on the mutant's hide. "And stay alert. Where there's one of these things, there could be more."

"I will be on guard," Rikki vowed, then ran into the woods again.

Hickok holstered the Colts and walked to the log. He found the girl huddled behind it. "You can come out now, little one. Blade took care of the icky thing."

Chastity rose tentatively. "He did?"

The gunman nodded at the corpse. "Take a gander for yourself."

She grinned at the sight of the dead mutant. "Blade must be real strong!" she marveled.

"Yep," Hickok agreed. "He lifts cows to keep in shape."

Chastity watched the giant finish wiping the blood from

his Bowies. He replaced them in their sheaths, then retrieved his M-16 and stepped over to the log.

"Is that the icky thing you saw?" Blade asked.

"Yes," Chastity said.

Blade sat down on the log, removed the spent magazine from his weapon, and withdrew a new mag from his left rear pocket. "You said you first saw the icky thing yesterday?"

"In the morning," Chastity disclosed.

"What were you doing when you saw it?" Blade casually inquired, inserting the fresh mag.

"I just woke up," Chastity said. "I was sleeping."

"Where?"

The girl pointed at the ground. "Right here. The icky thing was making noise and woke me up."

"It didn't see you?" Blade questioned.

Chastity shook her head. "It was over there." She indicated the south side of the clearing. "It went into the woods."

"Did you sleep here the whole night?" Blade inquired.

"Yes. I was afraid, so I stayed here after the icky thing left. Later the hairy pig came. And then all of you did."

"And you're by yourself?"

She frowned. "Yes."

Blade didn't want to upset the child by interrogating her about her mother. "Where's your father?" he asked.

"Daddy went to heaven."

Blade looked at Hickok, then at Chastity. "Do you mean he's dead?"

She nodded.

"How did he die?" Blade probed.

"I don't know."

"Then how do you know he's dead?"

"Mommy told me."

"What did she tell you?" Blade queried.

Chastity pondered for a few seconds. "Mommy said that daddy was killed—"

"Killed?" Blade interrupted. "Your mother used the

word 'killed'?"

"Yes," Chastity declared.

"Go on," Blade prompted.

"Mommy said daddy was killed 'cause of the Peers."

"The Peers? Who are the Peers?"

"They're the bad people!" Chastity stated.

Blade stared into her innocent eyes. "How far did you walk to get here?"

"I don't know. Far."

"Do you know how many days you were walking?" Blade asked, pressing her. "One? Two? More?"

"I don't remember," she replied. "After Mommy was burned, I walked a long, long time. And then I was standing on a hill all by myself, and I was really afraid. I walked some more, and walked and walked. Two days, maybe."

"Two days total, or two days after you were on the hill?"

"Two days after I was on the hill," Chastity answered.

"I don't suppose you know which direction you came from," Blade mentioned.

"No."

"North? South? East? West?"

"East!" Chastity exclaimed.

"You came from the east?" Blade inquired hopefully.

"No. Mommy told me the sun comes up in the east," Chastity said.

Blade sighed and gazed at the gunman. "Any suggestions? I don't see how we can retrace her route."

"Let me have a crack at it," Hickok said, leaning down. "Do you remember where you lived?"

"I sure do," Chastity responded.

"Okay. Was it a house in the country? Or did your family live in a city?"

"The city!" Chastity said excitedly. "We lived in the city!"

"Were there a heap of people there?" Hickok asked. "And lots of buildings?"

"Yes!"

"Do you know the name of this city?"

"Of course I do," she asserted with childlike conviction, as if the question were stupid.

"What's the name of it?"

Chastity smiled at them, proud of her memory. "Atlanta."

"Your family lives in Atlanta?" Blade interjected.

"We did."

Hickok patted her on the head. "Good girl. Now we know where to take you."

Chastity's eyes widened. "No!"

"You don't want to go back?" Blade observed.

"No!" she cried, taking a pace backwards. "I don't want to ever go back!"

"Why not?"

"It's a bad place! The Peers live there!"

"We wouldn't let the Peers do anything to you," Blade promised.

"No!" Chastity insisted. "I'll never go back! The Bubbleheads would get us!"

Blade motioned at the mutant and the boars. "We'd look out for you. Don't you think we could take care of you?"

"The Bubbleheads will burn you!"

"We must get to the bottom of this," Blade said.

"No!" Chastity repeated defiantly. "No!"

"Chastity . . ." Blade began.

"I won't go! I won't! I won't!"

Hickok straddled the log and lifted her to his chest. "Calm down, little one. No one is going to make you do something you don't want to do."

She stared at Blade accusingly, pouting. "What about him?"

Hickok smiled. "Don't pay any attention to him. He's just a fuddy-duddy."

"He sure is!" Chastity agreed.

The gunman was bending over to set her down when the question came.

"What's a fuddy-duddy?"

Chapter Four

"Was that wall there before the war, pard?"

"I don't remember reading anything about it," Blade replied.

Rikki cleared his throat. "I don't like the looks of this."

"I won't go down there! I won't!" Chastity mentioned yet again.

They were approximately 800 yards east of Atlanta, squatting in the cover of waist-high grass on the crest of a sloping mound. Hickok held Chastity on his left knee. The morning sun glistened off of windows and towering structures in the sprawling municipality.

"I had no idea it was so blamed big," Hickok remarked.

"Almost a million people lived there before the war," Blade said. "Atlanta was a major commercial and transportation center."

"What is it now?" Rikki asked.

"I didn't know Atlanta had skyscrapers," Hickok noted, gazing at a cluster of huge buildings in the center.

"We should be more concerned about the wall," Blade observed.

An enormous brick wall had been constructed around the city, enclosing Atlanta completely. At least 20 feet in height, the wall did not form a distinct geometric shape, but adhered to the contours of the land, skirting hills and other natural obstacles. A section might proceed straight for hundreds of yards, and then the wall would curve outward or inward for 50 to a hundred feet before resuming its direct course.

"I saw a picture of a wall like this once in a history book in the Family library," Hickok said. "What was it called?" He paused, pondering. "Oh, yeah. The Great Wall of China."

Blade grinned. "The Great Wall of China is much larger."

"Which one of us will venture into Atlanta?" Rikki inquired.

Blade gazed at a highway situated 200 yards to the north of their position. Which one indeed? They were all well rested, thanks to his decision to remain in the clearing overnight and catch up on their sleep. He had changed his mind about traveling when Chastity dozed off immediately after eating her supper. They were also well fed, thanks to the boar meat they'd consumed for their evening meal and for breakfast.

"None of us should mosey on down there," Hickok declared.

"One of us must go," Blade said. "I told you that last night."

"And I still think it's a mistake," the gunman asserted. "Let's take Chastity with us. Who cares who's in Atlanta?"

"I do," Blade responded. "And so should you. Chastity told us she has an aunt living in the city. We must try to find her."

"I won't go!" Chastity stressed.

"You'll stay here with Hickok," Blade instructed her. "I'm going into Atlanta."

"You're askin' for trouble," Hickok said.

"I agree," Rikki chimed in. "Why take the risk? Chastity doesn't want to go back. We should leave well enough alone."

"No can do," Blade mentioned. "We have a responsibility to her. We have a duty to try and locate her family."

"My mommy was my family," Chastity stated.

"What should we do while you're waltzin' around in Atlanta?" Hickok inquired.

Blade looked over his left shoulder at a stand of maple, dogwood, and hickory trees. "Hide in there. Wait for me."

Hickok sighed. "There's nothin' I can say to change your mind?"

"No."

The gunman stared at the city. "Then I'll go with you."

"No."

"Why not?" Hickok demanded.

"Chastity has taken a liking to you," Blade said. "She'll feel better if you stay."

"Then I'll go," Rikki offered.

"Nope."

"Give me one good reason?" Rikki said.

"We don't know what the setup is like," Blade noted. "One stranger might not attract too much attention. You can keep Hickok company."

"Please don't go," Chastity said.

"I'll be okay," Blade told her. He squinted at the skyscrapers. "Are weapons allowed in the city, Chastity?"

"Weapons?" she asked uncertainly.

"Yeah. Guns and knifes. Are the people allowed to carry weapons?"

"No," Chastity said. "No one carries them."

"What about the police force? Atlanta must have a police force," Blade remarked.

"The police have clubs," Chastity answered.

"What kind of clubs?" Blade quizzed her.

"Mommy said the police have clubs called blackjacks."

"What about the Bubbleheads?" Blade queried. "Are they police?"

"No," Chastity responded. "The Bubbleheads are . . ." She stopped, unable to recall the word her mother had frequently used.

"Do the Bubbleheads carry guns?"

"No."

Blade stroked his chin. "What about clothes?"

Chastity giggled. "Everybody wears clothes."

Hickok snickered.

"I know they wear clothes," Blade said. "But do they wear special clothes? Do they all wear outfits like yours?"

She shook her head. "Only Mommy," she said sadly.

Blade unslung the M-16 and rested the gun on the ground at his feet. He started to unbuckle his leather belt.

"You're not going in there unarmed?" Hickok asked in disbelief.

"How dumb do you think I am?" Blade answered, then added hastily, "Don't answer that!"

"Shucks," Hickok said.

Blade removed the Bowie sheaths from the belt, placed them next to his left foot, and looped his belt through his pants.

"Do you want to slip one of my Colts under your vest?" Hickok asked.

"No need," Blade replied. He raised the bottom of his left pants leg, then carefully wedged one of the Bowie sheaths under the top of his combat boot until the sheath and knife were secure.

"Sneaky," Hickok commented with a chuckle.

Blade repeated the procedure with the other Bowie, jamming the sheath under his right combat boot.

"What if you're searched?" Rikki brought up.

"I'll cross that bridge when I come to it," Blade said, smoothing both of his pants legs down. "You two watch my M-16."

"Look!" Chastity exclaimed, pointing at the highway.

Blade swiveled, surprised to see four figures moving toward Atlanta. Traffic on the highway, vehicular or otherwise, was sparse. He'd observed two cars and one man afoot during the hour they'd spent watching the metropolis. The lone traveler had been an elderly man dressed in tattered clothing. These four were quite different. Their garments were a unique, shimmering silver, composed of a fabric that reflected the brilliant sunshine and cast the four figures in an unearthly radiance.

"The Bubbleheads!" Chastity cried, recoiling in Hickok's arms.

"Those are the Bubbleheads?" Blade remarked, peering at the dazzling forms intently. Even their heads and hands shone, and there appeared to be objects on their backs.

Hickok hugged Chastity. "They can't see us," he said, trying to comfort her. "You're safe."

She buried her face in his chest. "They burned my mom."

"They won't burn you."

Chastity's narrow shoulders moved up and down.

Hickok looked at Blade, then at the Bubbleheads. "Those rotten coyotes."

"Are they humans or mutants?" Rikki inquired of no one in particular.

"I'll let you know," Blade said, and slipped away through the grass, heading for the highway.

Hickok kept his worried eyes on his friend until the giant was lost to view in the undergrowth. He frowned, hearing Chastity sniffle, and glanced at Rikki. "This stinks."

"Blade will be back," the martial artist responded.

Chastity unexpectedly straightened and swung her head around. Tears streaked her cheeks. "Where's Blade?"

"On his way into Atlanta," Hickok informed her.

"Don't let him!" she stated in alarm.

"There's nothing we can do about it," Hickok said.

"Please! The Bubbleheads will get him!"

Hickok gazed into her earnest eyes, impressed by the terror her features conveyed. "There's nothing Rikki and I can do," he reiterated. "Blade is the head Warrior. We're flunkies. Whatever he says, goes."

"Flunkies?"

"Blade is our boss," Hickok clarified. "He gives us orders, and it's our job to follow them."

"He tells you what to do?" Chastity said. "Like my mommy always told me?"

The gunfighter smiled. "Something like that. You see, at the place we come from, called the Home, there are eighteen Warriors who protect everybody else. Blade is in charge of all the Warriors. We work under him.''

Chastity wiped her eyes with the back of her right hand. ''I'm sorry.''

''For what?''

''For crying.''

''There's no need to apologize,'' Hickok said.

''But Mommy said I should keep quiet 'cause of the Bubbleheads,'' Chastity explained.

''The Bubbleheads are too far off to hear us,'' Hickok told her.

Chastity relaxed and stared at Atlanta. ''Where is the place you live?''

''A long way from here,'' Hickok replied.

''Is it nice?''

''I think so. The folks livin' at the Home are decent people.''

''Do they hurt each other?'' Chastity asked, looking at him.

''Now and then,'' Hickok admitted. ''But for the most part, they treat each other kindly.''

''We try to live by the Golden Rule,'' Rikki interjected.

''What rule?'' Chastity wanted to learn.

''We do to others as we would have them do to us,'' Rikki detailed. ''We try to live Spirit-led lives.''

''What's that?''

''Did your mother instruct you in the ways of the Spirit?'' Rikki asked.

''Do you mean God?''

Rikki nodded.

''Oh, sure. Mom told me all about God. She whispered.''

Rikki's forehead furrowed in perplexity. ''Why did she whisper?''

'' 'Cause you're not allowed to talk about God,'' Chastity said.

''It's illegal to talk about God?'' Rikki inquired in amazement.

''Yes,'' Chastity confirmed. ''But Mommy told me about

God anyway. God lives in a big house in the sky, and he loves everyone, and he likes harp music.''

Rikki smiled. ''Your mother must have been very religious.''

''She loved God,'' Chastity said, the corners of her mouth drooping. She sniffed loudly.

Hickok glared at the martial artist and silently mouthed the word ''Idiot!'' Then he quickly changed the subject. ''Do you know I have a little guy about your age?''

''You do?''

''Yep. His name is Ringo, and he's a chip off the old block.''

''Ringo?'' Chastity said, and laughed. ''Another funny name!''

''Our names are funny?'' Hickok responded.

Chastity nodded. ''I never heard your names before. Hickok. Ringo. And Ricky-Tickle-Taffy.''

Hickok had to cover his mouth with his left hand to suppress his mirth.

''It's Rikki-Tikki-Tavi,'' the martial artist told her.

''It's still funny,'' Chastity said. ''Where did you get it?''

''I selected my name.''

''Your mommy and daddy didn't give you your name?'' Chastity inquired, astonished.

''They gave me a name at birth,'' Rikki answered.

''What was it?''

''Brandon.''

''Then why isn't your name Brandon?''

''I'll try and explain,'' Rikki said patiently. ''At our Home, when we turn sixteen, we are allowed to pick a new name for our very own. Any name we want.''

''Why?''

''The man who founded our Home started the practice,'' Rikki replied. ''He wanted his followers to never forget about the war, about the reasons the human race almost destroyed itself. He believed history was very important. So he asked all of his followers to go through the history books and pick any name they wanted as their very own

on their sixteenth birthday.'' He paused. ''Now we select
our names from any source. We call this ceremony our
Naming. I picked the name of a mongoose.''

''What's a mongoose?''

''Do you know what a ferret is?''

''No.''

''Well, a mongoose and a ferret are a lot alike. They're
about the size of a cat.''

''What's a cat?''

''You've never seen a cat?''

''Nope.''

Rikki looked at Hickok.

''Don't they have cats in Atlanta?'' the gunman inquired.

''Nope.''

''What about dogs?'' Hickok asked.

''Nope.''

''Are there *any* animals in Atlanta?''

Chastity shook her head.

''No one has a pet?'' Hickok questioned skeptically.

''No,'' Chastity answered. ''The Bubbleheads get you
if you have an animal.''

Hickok gazed at the city thoughtfully. ''The Big Guy
shouldn't be down there by his lonesome.''

''The Bubbleheads will get him,'' Chastity said.

''He won't be caught,'' Hickok stated.

''He will,'' Chastity insisted. ''They'll know he isn't a
Citizen.''

Hickok locked his eyes on hers. ''What are you talkin'
about?''

''His clothes.''

The gunman gripped her shoulders. ''What about his
clothes? You said the people don't wear special clothes,
that they don't wear outfits like yours.''

''Not *blue* ones.''

Hickok grit his teeth as he glanced at the metropolis.

''Blue was the only color we could wear,'' Chastity went
on. ''Blue was the color for our class, Mom said.''

''And the other folks?''

''Everyone wears different colors.''

"But are the clothes all styled like yours?" Rikki interrupted.

"They're all pretty much the same," Chastity verified.

"Blast!" Hickok declared, pounding the ground in frustration.

Chastity, startled, cringed. "Did I say something wrong?"

"No, little lady," Hickok told her, and looked at Rikki. "Do you want to flip for it?"

For an answer, Rikki-Tikki-Tavi rose and raced toward the highway.

Chapter Five

Blade halted behind the last tree before the highway and looked in both directions. The Bubbleheads were 50 feet to his right, heading for the wall, now 500 yards distant. To his left the road was deserted. He decided to keep hidden until the four silver figures were closer to the city.

A bird was chirping across the highway.

The Warrior heard the rumble of a motor coming from the city and crouched alongside the trunk. He spied a green car speeding toward the Bubbleheads, and watched as the vehicle rapidly covered the intervening span and braked. The silver forms climbed inside and the car executed a U-turn and retraced its route, returning to the open gate and vanishing within. The gate was promptly closed.

Blade stood and walked to the highway, then made for Atlanta. He adopted a nonchalant attitude, strolling along as if he didn't have a care in the world. All the while he scrutinized the wall. He wanted to enter the city without a hitch, but he spotted several problems as he drew nearer. Foremost was a metal gate limiting access to the metropolis, with six guards, all of whom were wearing dark blue uniforms, posted outside to screen entrants. Three additional guards were on the rampart above the gate.

This was not good.

He should have asked Chastity whether the people of Atlanta were required to carry indentification cards. If so, he wouldn't make it past the gate. He toyed with the notion of ducking into the brush, but he noticed that the guards on the rampart were regarding him critically. They might sound an alarm if he acted suspiciously. His best bet was to hope he could bluff his way into the city.

From somewhere deep within Atlanta a siren wailed.

Blade advanced boldly, never slackening his pace. He saw the six guards fan out the width of the road, blocking the gate, and he knew they would stop him. Undaunted, he continued, and when he was within 60 yards of the waiting men in blue he noticed one other person near the gate, sitting on the left side, back to the wall.

A person he'd seen earlier.

The elderly man in the bedraggled clothes.

One of the guards took two strides forward, his hands on his hips.

Blade smiled as he approached the men in blue. None of the guards sported firearms. Every man, though, had a thin leather holster attacked to his belt, some with the holster on their right hip, others on their left.

The guard in front was a burly character with bushy brows and a glowering countenance.

Blade glanced at the elderly man, who was observing him sadly. Why?

"Halt!" the burly guard barked when the giant was ten yards off.

Blade complied.

"Raise your arms straight out and turn around slowly," the guard directed.

The Warrior obeyed.

"Okay, stranger," the guard said when the giant had made a complete revolution. "Come here."

Blade walked to within a foot of the head guard. "Hello," he said pleasantly.

"Where are you from?" the man demanded.

Obviously, they knew he wasn't from Atlanta. "I'm from Miami," Blade replied.

"Miami, huh?" the guard commented. "We get about

a dozen from the Miami area each year. What's your business in Atlanta?''

"I'm trying to find a cousin of mine," Blade lied.

"You have a relative here?''

"I was told that my cousin lives here," Blade answered. "Maybe you know her. Her name is Llewellyn Snow.''

"The name doesn't ring a bell," the man said. "What's yours?''

"Jack. Jack Snow.''

"Well, Mr. Snow," the guard stated, "I'm Officer Connery. And I'm going to tell you how it is. Although you're not a Citizen of Atlanta, you're entitled to certain rights by decree of the Civil Council. You have the right to an attorney at any time. Should you violate a law, you have the right to a preliminary hearing within twenty-four hours of the offense. Bear in mind, an accused person is always considered guilty until proven innocent. This—''

"Guilty until proven innocent?" Blade repeated. He had the impression Officer Connery was reciting memorized information. "Isn't that backwards? Before the war, a person was viewed as innocent until proven guilty.''

Officer Connery studied the giant. "You must be literate.''

"I can read," Blade acknowledged.

"Be sure and tell that to your Escort," Officer Connery suggested. "If you decide to apply for Citizenship Status, it will be a plus in your favor.''

"My Escort?''

"Every visitor to Atlanta is assigned an official escort," Officer Connery said. "The Escort will be with you at all times. After all"—he smiled—"we wouldn't want you to wander around by yourself and get lost.''

"How very thoughtful," Blade noted dryly.

"Now where was I?" Connery commented. "Oh, yes. An accused person is always considered guilty until proven innocent. This is because the Civil Rights of the majority outweigh the rights of any one individual.''

Blade listened in fascination, now convinced the officer was giving a standard speech, one delivered by rote to each newcomer.

"If you have any questions, ask your Escort," Officer Connery said. "All visitors are granted a forty-eight-hour stay in Atlanta. Should you desire to stay longer, you must receive permission. Ask your Escort about the procedure."

"Will the Escort help me find my cousin?"

"Yes," Connery answered. "Your Escort is at your service. Anything you need, the Escort will provide. The Citizens of Atlanta want your stay here to be a happy, memorable experience."

"I didn't expect such courtesy," Blade mentioned.

"Those who serve are those who are happy," Connery remarked as if he was quoting from a book.

"Where do I meet my Escort?"

"Wait over there," Officer Connery instructed, pointing at the elderly man sitting to the left of the gate. "A patrol will conduct you to the Visitors Bureau in the Civil Directorate in a few minutes. You will be assigned to an Escort there."

"Thanks," Blade said, and took a stride toward the wall.

"Just a moment," Officer Connery declared, holding aloft his right hand. "There's one more thing."

"What?"

"You must be frisked. Weapons are not allowed in Atlanta. You can declare any arms here, and they will be held until you are ready to leave the city. Do you have any to declare?"

Blade hesitated. If he said yes, they would take his Bowies, leaving him unarmed. If he told them no, they might discover the knives while frisking him and confiscate them or refuse to admit him, or both. There were only six, and he was confident he could take care of them if violence erupted. He glanced at the three on the rampart, startled to observe AR-15s in their hands. Where did the guns come from? Chastity had claimed the police force carried black-

jacks, which explained the thin leather holsters on the six
officers outside the gate. Was Chastity mistaken, or did
only the wall guards use AR-15s and she was unaware of
it? This changed the entire situation. If he said no and they
found the Bowies, they might shoot him on the spot. Better
to lose the knives than risk death or imprisonment. But
before he could open his mouth to reply, Officer Connery
reached out and patted his waist.

"This won't take long," Connery mentioned.

The Warrior tensed as the officer's hands expertly probed
his belt and roamed over his black leather vest.

"Most travelers do carry weapons," Officer Connery
remarked. "Although someone your size might not need
any." He leaned down, his hands pressing against the
giant's pockets, feeling for a pocketknife or a derringer.

Blade casually gazed up at the trio on the rampart.

"The crime rate is very low here," Connery went on.
"The Orientation and Community Directorates see to that."

"What are they?" Blade asked, girding himself to make
a bid to escape into the nearby forest.

"Your Escort will explain everything," Officer Connery
said, lowering his hands to the giant's knees.

Blade focused on the right side of the officer's neck. A
single, well-placed strike should do the trick.

Connery's hands hovered inches from the Warrior's
ankles.

There was a sudden commotion at the gate as a half-dozen
men in blue marched up to the metal bars. The gate was
arranged with the vertical bars spaced six inches apart and
with thicker horizontal bars at the top and bottom. A huge,
square lock secured the two sections in the center.

"Sergeant Connery! Open up!" a tall man with a clipped
brown mustache and short brown hair bellowed.

Connery straightened and stood. "Yes, sir." He hurried
over, produced a key ring from his right front pocket, and
unlocked the gate. "You're five minutes early, Captain."
He grabbed one of the vertical bars and pulled the gate
open.

"There were no visitors at the other gates," the captain commented as he stepped out, his brown eyes raking the giant. "Who is this?"

"Mr. Jack Snow," Officer Connery answered. "He's here looking for a relative."

The captain nodded. "Pleased to meet you. I'm Captain Yost." He caught sight of the elderly man and frowned.

"Long time no see, Yost," the elderly man said sarcastically.

"Glisson!" Captain Yost snapped. "I'd given you up for dead."

"Not yet."

"What are you doing here?" Captain Yost questioned.

"The usual."

"Once a leech, always a leech," Captain Yost declared.

"Is that any way for a Citizen to talk to a visitor?" Glisson retorted.

Captain Yost took a stride toward Glisson. "Have a care, old man. And I do mean *old*." He paused. "How old are you, anyway?"

"Sixty-four."

"Do tell?" Captain Yost grinned and looked at Blade. "We will take you to the Visitors Bureau."

"Thank you."

Captain Yost motioned for Blade and Glisson to precede him through the gate. "After you."

The man called Glisson rose slowly and shuffled forward. "If it's any consolation, Captain," he said, "the last thing I ever wanted to do was come back here."

"Are you becoming noble in your old age?" Yost cracked.

Glisson walked inside, his lean frame stooped at the waist, his shoulders hunched. His brown shoes were cracked and discolored, his tan pants sported ragged holes on both knees, and his olive shirt had seen better days decades ago.

Blade waited until Glisson entered, then followed.

Captain Yost was last. He turned and addressed the

sergeant. "Keep your eyes peeled. The OCI has received word of a rebel band in the area."

"Has the report been confirmed?" Officer Connery asked.

"No," Captain Yost said. "But you never can tell."

"We'll stay alert," Officer Connery promised.

"You'd better," Yost declared. "It's your ass if you don't." The five men with him had formed into a straight file and were standing at attention, facing the inner city, the skyscrapers on the horizon. He moved to the lead position, then glanced at Blade and Glisson. "Follow us. And don't stray." So saying, he waved his right arm and the squad began to march to the west.

Blade tramped on the last patrolman's heels.

Glisson kept pace on the giant's right. "So this is your first visit to Atlanta?" he inquired after they had covered 15 yards.

"Yes," Blade confirmed.

"I couldn't help overhearing your conversation with Connery," Glisson remarked.

Blade was busy surveying his surroundings, his first glimpse of the metropolis close up. Trees lined the road. They were in a residential area, with immaculately maintained frame homes and neatly trimmed lawns. Children played in the front yards. Sidewalks bordered the asphalt, but Yost was leading his men along the right side of the road, next to the curb. There was no vehicular traffic.

"Do you know anything about Atlanta?" Glisson queried in a low tone.

"Not much."

"Do you plan to stay here after you locate your relative?" Glisson asked.

Blade glanced at the man. "Why all the questions?"

Glisson looked at the backs of the squad, then at the giant. "I'm not being nosy. No, sir! A person doesn't live to my age by prying into the affairs of others."

Blade spotted two youngsters tossing a blue ball.

"If you want to stay here, that's fine by me," Glisson continued. "I'm not about to tell anyone what to do."

"How many times have you been here?" Blade inquired.

"I've lost count," Glisson said.

"If you like Atlanta so much, why don't you live here?"

Glisson snickered. "I wouldn't be talking to you right now if I'd lived here."

"I don't understand," Blade admitted.

"You will."

The road curved to the north, then angled westward again. A panoramic vista of the city spread before them, the skyscrapers rearing skyward at the very heart of Atlanta. Approximately a mile from the center of the municipality, in contrast to the older edifices, loomed seven eerie silver structures, ten-story monoliths constructed of a lustrous synthetic.

"What are those?" Blade asked in amazement. From a distance, from beyond the outer wall, the monoliths had blended into the skyline, indistinguishable and unexceptional.

"They're the Directorates," Glisson disclosed.

"Do people live there?"

"No," Glisson said, chuckling. "The Directorates are government buildings."

"Why are there so many?"

"Each Directorate is diffferent," Glisson said. "Each one has a separate function." He paused and scratched his grizzled chin. "Let's see. There's the Civil Directorate, the Ethics Directorate, the Community Directorate, the Euthanasia Directorate, the Life Directorate, the Progress Directorate, and the Orientation Directorate." He smiled. "Damn! I remembered them all!"

"Is the mayor in the Civil Directorate?"

"The mayor?"

"I read about city governments," Blade said. "Most cities were governed by a mayor."

Glisson laughed and shook his head. "Mister, that was

ages ago, before the war, when there was such a thing as democracy. Times have changed. Most cities are city-states, and democracy died with the launching of the missiles.''

"There are a few pockets of democracy left," Blade mentioned.

"They're few and far between," Glisson said. "And Atlanta isn't one of them." He glanced at the squad, at Captain Yost, dread flitting across his features.

"So who is in charge of Atlanta?"

"The Peers."

"And who are they?" Blade questioned.

"The seven heads of the Directorates," Glisson replied.

"They run the show?" Blade remarked.

"Mister, they *are* the show. They control the whole shebang. Whatever they say, goes." Glisson stared at the monoliths and shuddered. "The seven Peers, collectively, are called the Civil Council. If you like being healthy, don't ever cross them."

"How are these Peers picked? Are they elected by the people?" Blade probed.

Glisson snickered. "Elected? Don't make me laugh! The Peers are appointed for life. Whenever a vacancy occurs, the remaining members get together and pick a replacement. This way, they can keep it in the family."

"I don't understand," Blade admitted.

The elderly man studied the giant. "They sure grow 'em stupid where you come from."

"Bear with me," Blade said. "This is my first time here, remember?"

"And it could be your last," Glisson muttered.

Blade gazed at four children playing in a nearby yard. "Atlanta seems peaceful enough to me."

"Looks can be deceiving," Glisson responded.

"Are you sure that you're not exaggerating?"

"May God strike me . . ." Glisson began, abruptly stopping as the patrol came to a sudden halt.

Captain Yost was holding his right arm aloft and glancing over his left shoulder at Glisson.

"Damn!" Glisson muttered. "I'm in for it now."

Captain Yost smiled maliciously as he strolled toward the old man.

"I didn't do anything," Glisson blurted.

Yost halted, his smile widening. "I had no idea you want to become an Escort."

Glisson did a double take. "What the hell are you talking about? The last thing I would do is kiss ass for a living."

"Don't be shy," Captain Yost said. "If you want to be an Escort, I'll put in a word for you." He chuckled.

Blade listened to the exchange in perplexity. Yost was baiting Glisson for some reason. Obviously, the good captain disliked the elderly gent intensely. But why?

"What game are you playing?" Glisson demanded. "I'll never be an Escort and you know it."

"You could have fooled me," Captain Yost stated bitterly. "You've been acting just like an Escort for Mr. Snow here. I'm impressed by your knowledge of Atlanta's governmental structure. I really am. I didn't think your pea brain was capable of retaining anything."

"Screw you!"

Captain Yost made a smacking noise with his tongue. "How typically crude! And I was trying to be nice!"

"Why don't you shove a broom up your butt?" Glisson snapped. "It might improve your disposition."

Yost straightened and clasped his hands behind his back. "I have you, you bastard! After all these years I have you!"

"I know my rights!" Glisson exclaimed.

"Good," Yost sneered. "Where I'm taking you, a knowledge of your rights will come in handy." He laughed.

Glisson gulped and glanced at the monoliths. "Where are you taking me?"

Captain Yost ignored the question and looked at the giant. "I trust you will bear with me. We must make a slight detour, and then I will conduct you to the Civil Directorate."

"Where are you taking me?" Glisson asked anxiously.

Yost faced the man in the tattered clothing. "Where else,

you lying degenerate? You're not sixty-four. You're sixty-seven.''

Glisson took a step backwards, his right hand rising to his throat. "You knew?"

Captain Yost nodded. "I've been waiting to nail your ass for a long time! I despise leeches like you." He paused. "No, you won't be freeloading off the citizens of Atlanta any more. You're not going to the Civil Directorate."

"No!" Glisson cried.

"Yes," Captain Yost said, gloating. "I'm taking you to Euthanasia."

Chapter Six

In his eagerness to reach Blade and warn his colossal companion not to enter Atlanta, Rikki-Tikki-Tavi was uncharacteristically careless. He dashed through the undergrowth, angling toward the road, certain he would overtake Blade easily.

He didn't count on the pit.

Rikki reached a wide clearing halfway between Hickok's position on the rise and the highway. The Uzi flapped against his right shoulder and his katana scabbard bumped his left thigh. He gripped the hilt of his cherished sword to keep the weapon in place, his eyes surveying the vegetation ahead for the clearest path. In two more bounds the trap was sprung. His left foot landed and started to sink as the ground buckled under his weight. He realized his mistake, gauged the danger, and reacted in milliseconds; even as his left leg sagged he was throwing himself into the air, launching his steely form as far forward as he could manage, hoping his outstretched fingers would find a purchase on solid turf.

He was almost successful.

The martial artist struck the opposite rim with a jarring impact, his forearms hooking on the lip as his body slammed into the hard side. With the crackle of breaking branches and the swish of falling grass mats, the makeshift pit cover collapsed. Rikki dangled from the top, his fingers clawing at the earth, his feet seeking a foothold. Whoever had constructed the trap had known what they were doing; the inner surface was smooth and unyielding.

His hands were his only chance.

Rikki dug his fingernails into the dirt, grimacing at the strain, feeling himself slipping backwards, his mind filled with a vision of poison-tipped stakes waiting to skewer him. Slowly, inexorably, he was losing his grip.

Heavy footsteps sounded to his left. Two pairs of brown leather boots appeared, and stopped inches from his hands.

"Hold it!" someone declared in a low tone.

"What is it?" responded the second man. "Let's waste the scum and be done with it."

"Take a look," urged the first speaker.

There was a moment of silence.

"Son of a bitch!" exclaimed the second one.

Rikki glanced upward to discover two men dressed in green. Both were armed with long bows. The larger of the duo was aiming an arrow at his face.

"You get him out, Dale," said the larger man. "I'll cover you."

The one called Dale, a young man with blond hair and blue eyes, nodded. He slung his long bow over his right shoulder and grasped Rikki's wrists. "Be still, stranger," he directed. "I'll have you out in a jiffy. Just don't give John cause to let fly."

John backed up, his sturdy arms steady as he kept the arrow trained on the man in black.

Rikki allowed himself to be drawn from the pit. A moment later he was on his hands and knees, and Dale had moved to the left and drawn a ten-inch survival knife. Rikki realized they each had a camouflage sheath on their right hip.

"On your feet," Dale directed.

"And be quick about it," John added brusquely.

Rikki rose, careful to keep his hands away from his weapons.

"Let the Uzi drop," John ordered.

Rikki complied.

"Now the fancy sword," John directed.

The Warrior hesitated.

"Do it or die," the big man said, wagging the tip of the arrow.

"I want this back," Rikki asserted as he drew the scabbard from under his belt and lowered it to the grass.

"You shouldn't be worried about your sword," John mentioned. "You should be concerned about your life."

Dale stepped in and scooped up both weapons. "We must get out of here."

"I can't leave," Rikki said calmly.

John snorted. "You don't have any choice."

"But I must—" Rikki began.

"Move!" John barked, indicating the forest to their right with a jerk of the bow. "Not another word out of you or you're buzzard meat!"

Rikki knew the big man meant every word. He frowned and turned, walking across the clearing with his captors on his heels. Now what? If he didn't escape soon, Blade would be in serious trouble. He *had* to prevent Blade from entering Atlanta. But how?

"Head east," John ordered.

Rikki followed the big man's instructions. "I would like to speak," he said after 15 yards.

"Save it," John responded.

"A friend of mine is in jeopardy."

"Sure," John said sarcastically.

"I'm serious," Rikki insisted.

"Save it for Locklin," John advised.

"I would be in your debt if you would permit me to go to my friend," Rikki said.

"You're not going anywhere."

Dale cleared his throat. "I think he's telling the truth."

"So what if he is?" John countered. "Locklin told us to watch the pit and use our judgment on the catch. You're the one who stopped me from killing this clown. If it'd been up to me—''

"Look at his clothes," Dale declared. "It's obvious he isn't a trooper. He's certainly not a Terminator. I doubt he's from the city."

"You're too gullible, kid," John commented.

"Don't call me kid."

John sighed. "Look. Maybe this guy is telling the truth. But we're not about to let him go. We'll take him to Locklin. The boss will know what to do with him."

"How far must we travel?" Rikki inquired.

"You'll know when we get there," John replied.

Rikki looked back. They were staying six feet away, too far to reach before John unleashed his arrow. And Dale had put the survival knife away and was holding the Uzi with his finger on the trigger. The katana was secured under Dale's brown belt.

"Keep your eyes front," John said.

Frustrated, the Warrior frowned as he marched eastward. Every stride took him farther from Blade. He hoped Chastity had been wrong, that Blade would not be arrested simply for wearing a different type of attire than the people of Atlanta.

"What's your name?" Dale asked.

"Rikki-Tikki-Tavi."

The big man snickered. "What kind of a name is that?"

Rikki didn't bother to answer.

"Where are you from?" Dale inquired.

"Far from Atlanta."

"Where exactly?" Dale probed.

"I can't say."

"Why not?" John retorted. "Don't you trust us?" He chuckled at his joke.

"Why have you captured me?" Rikki questioned. "I came here in peace."

"Why are you here?" Dale wanted to know.

"I can't say."

"Locklin will make you talk," John declared.

"Are you scavengers?" Rikki asked, hoping to elicit more information.

"Scavengers?" John exploded. "We're not slime-sucking scavengers, you smart-ass."

"Thieves then?"

"One more insult, buster, and I'll part your hair with my shaft," John warned.

"What else can you be?" Rikki asked. "Unless digging a pit is your way of meeting people."

"Funny man," John said.

"We dug the pit to catch police or Terminators," Dale disclosed. "The Peers are always sending them after us."

"Who are the Peers?"

"If you don't know who the Peers are, you can't be from Atlanta," Dale stated.

"I told you I wasn't," Rikki reminded him.

"Quit flapping your gums and keep walking," John interjected.

Rikki scrutinized the terrain ahead, searching for an advantageous spot. He wasn't about to let the men in green take him miles from his companions, and he intended to turn the tables at the first opportunity.

"Are you from Memphis?" the youthful Dale queried.

"No," Rikki said.

"We're heard about the men in black in Memphis," Dale commented. "I thought you might be one of them."

"I've never been to Memphis," Rikki elaborated.

"Me neither," Dale said wistfully. "I've never been more than fifty miles from Atlanta, and I'd like to travel. But I can't leave, not until the Peers are eliminated and the people of Atlanta are free once again."

Rikki looked at Dale. "You are revolutionaries?"

"We're Freedom Fighters!" John thundered. "We'll make the Peers pay for their crimes! For every child they've killed, for every senior citizen they've put to sleep, they're going to pay!"

"You intend to overthrow the rulers of Atlanta," Rikki deduced.

"Butchers, you mean!" John declared.

"You must forgive Big John," Dale said. "His passion gets the better of him."

Big John's emotions were, indeed, taxing his self-control to the breaking point. His thick lips were clenched and twitching, and he lowered the bow a few inches as he glared at the Warrior.

Rikki's eyes narrowed as he recognized the opening he needed. "Is your cause just?" he casually inquired.

"Just?" Big John responded, halting and lowering the bow several more inches.

Rikki stopped and pivoted, his hands at his sides.

"Is it just to fight dictators who control an entire city?" Big John demanded. "Is it just to want to put an end to the slaughter of fetuses and the elderly? Is it just to want freedom for all?"

Dale was standing to Big John's right, listening attentively, the Uzi pointed downward.

Rikki took a measured step nearer the big man. "I know a little about Freedom Fighters," he mentioned. "We studied them in our history class at my Home. Before the war there were two types. One was legitimate, men and women who genuinely believed in the right of everyone to be free of all tyranny. The second type was a sham. They were usually Communists who were trying to overthrow an established government. They would spread death and destruction, claiming to be solely interested in securing freedom for the people, when their main objective was to subjugate the very people they professed to be helping. Which kind are you?"

Big John took a stride closer, his cheeks reddening. "You're comparing us to the lousy Commies? I should stomp you into the dust!"

Rikki shrugged and held his hands at waist height, palms up. "I was merely making a point."

"Well, we're not Commies," Big John declared angrily.

"So you say," Rikki observed, deliberately taunting him.

John moved to within a foot of the man in black, the long bow held in front of him. "Are you calling me a liar?"

"No," Rikki said. "But foolish." So saying, he went into action with a cool, detached efficiency, wanting to dispatch the duo without causing them grievous harm. His right foot swept up and in, catching Big John on the left shin. The big bowman instinctively doubled over in surprise and pain, and Rikki pressed his initiative. He speared his right hand into John's groin.

Gasping and gurgling, John tried to cover his privates with his right hand.

As Rikki expected.

The Warrior brought his hands around in an arc, gouging his fingers into John's neck.

Big John coughed and sputtered and fell onto his left knee.

Stunned by the unexpectedness of the martial artist's assault, Dale had gaped as Rikki easily handled his associate. Now he took a frantic pace forward, raising the Uzi.

Rikki-Tikki-Tavi sidestepped the panting big man and leaped into the air, flawlessly performing a devastating spinning-wheel kick. He intentionally reduced the amount of force he applied, and instead of breaking Dale's neck he clipped the rash youth on the chin.

Dale was knocked onto his back by the blow, dazed.

Rikki came down in the Zenkutsu-tachi, the forward stance, and rotated, clipping Big John on the back of the head with the ball of his right foot.

The big man toppled over like a downed oak.

As much as he would have liked to interrogate the two men, Rikki was impatient to return to the highway and ascertain whether Blade had already entered Atlanta. He retrieved his katana, sliding the scabbard under his belt, and reached for the Uzi.

"I wouldn't, friend, if I were you."

Rikki glanced up at the sound of the resonant voice, to his right, his right arm frozen in midair.

"If you touch that gun, you're dead."

The speaker was a lean man in green apparel. Neatly clipped red hair crowned his handsome features. A full red mustache framed his upper lip, and a jutting, trim red beard projected from his angular chin. A long bow was slung over his back, but he made no move to touch it.

He didn't need to.

Dozens of men and women in green encircled the Warrior, all of them with bows, some with long bows, others with crossbows, and a few with compounds. Every one of the archers was training an arrow on the man in black.

"If you don't mind, put your sword on the ground," said the man with the red hair. "And if you do mind, then I'm afraid my band will see fit to turn you into a pincushion."

Chapter Seven

Euthanasia? What in the world was Euthanasia? Blade racked his memory, knowing he'd seen the word before, but he couldn't recall its meaning. He saw Glisson turn white as the proverbial sheet. Captain Yost was chuckling triumphantly.

"I won't go!" Glisson cried. "You can't make me."

"Want to bet?" Captain Yost retorted.

"It's against the law," Glisson said. "Only citizens are permitted to be officially extinguished."

Captain Yost grinned. "Not any more." He paused. "You've been gone a long time, and you would have been better off if you'd stayed away. During your absence the Civil Council amended the Euthanasia Directorate's admissions policy. And guess what?"

"They can't!" Glisson protested.

"They can and they will," Captain Yost stated. "Anyone sixty-six or older is automatically admitted to Euthanasia. After your last visit, I went to records and had them run a computer check on you. That's how I discovered your age. Frankly, I was surprised to see you show up here again."

"A man's got to eat," Glisson said.

"Where you're going, you won't need food," Yost noted.

Blade ventured to intervene on the elderly man's behalf.

"Does this have anything to do with the conversation Glisson and I had?"

"Not really," Captain Yost answered. "I did overhear parts of your talk. You'd be smart to forget everything he told you. He's a borderline rebel."

"I am not," Glisson said, disputing the officer.

"By law," Captain Yost went on, disregarding Glisson's comment, "indigents have their rights too. Until two months ago, the Civil Directorate was required to temporarily feed and clothe all destitute persons, even bums who showed up at our gates begging for a handout." He looked at Glisson. "Case in point."

"I've never begged for anything in my life," Glisson said.

"We're tired of letting freeloaders leech off us," Captain Yost declared.

"Listen," Glisson said, "you can keep your rotten food and moth ridden clothes. Who needs them? Just let me go."

"Do you hear this bum?" Yost asked Blade. "He has the gall to show up every now and then for a free handout, for hot meals and new clothes, and then he hits the road again. His type has no redeeming social value."

"That's me," Glisson agreed. "Now will you let me go?"

Captain Yost fixed a baleful gaze on the old man. "Not on your life. I told you. The Civil Council has extended the Euthanasia Direcorate's authority to include indigents. And according to the records, you're sixty-six." He smirked. "Are you ready for the Sleeper?"

Glisson abruptly whirled and took off as fast as his spindly legs would carry him.

Blade took a step after him.

"Don't waste your energy," Captain Yost said. He motioned with his right arm. "Get him!" he barked.

The five policemen sprinted in pursuit of the fleeing Glisson.

"I don't know where the fool thinks he's going," Captain Yost observed sarcastically.

Blade was trying to comprehend the situation, sorting the information he'd learned. The government of Atlanta was administered by seven Directorates. The heads of the Directorates—the seven Peers, as they styled themselves—formed an executive body known as the Civil Council. They were ultimately responsible for running the city. But what was this business about being 66 years old? And he still couldn't recall the definition of "euthanasia."

The five troopers in blue had caught up with Glisson.

"Once the social parasites are disposed of, we'll have the perfect society," Captain Yost commented.

"Disposed of?"

Captain Yost nodded. "That's what the Sleeper Chambers are for. Eternal oblivion."

Blade suddenly remembered the meaning of "euthanasia." It was the act of putting someone to death! "Glisson will be killed?" he queried, shocked.

"Killed is the wrong word," Captain Yost said. "Think of it as a mercy disposition."

"Euthanasia is permitted in Atlanta?" Blade questioned.

"Hell, it's encouraged," Captain Yost answered.

"I don't understand," Blade admitted.

"What's to understand?" Captain Yost responded. "American society was leaning toward officially sanctioned euthanasia before the war. We've simply put into effect a practice they lacked the balls to implement. Mercy dispositions are essential to a well-managed society. Once citizens have outlived their usefulness, why keep them around to burden everyone else?"

"Here he is, sir," one of the men in blue announced as they returned. Two of them were supporting Glisson, their hands holding his upper arms.

"Let me go, damn you!" Glisson snapped.

"Save your breath," Captain Yost said. "Bring him," he directed his men. Then he turned to Blade. "Again, I apologize for the slight delay. Please come with me." The officer wheeled and headed toward the monoliths.

Blade fell in beside Yost. He saw citizens on both

sidewalks, and he noticed they were all wearing jumpsuits of varying colors. Some wore light blue jumpsuits exactly like Chastity's, while others worn brown or green. With the singular exception of the dark blue uniforms the police were wearing, everyone was attired in jumpsuits. Why?

"I take it you don't approve of our mercy dispositions," Captain Yost commented.

"No," Blade said.

"Why not?"

"How can you justify killing innocent people?"

"Who says they're innocent?" Captain Yost rejoined. "If they have outlived their usefulness, then they're guilty of existing at the expense of the productive members of society."

"Might makes right, eh?" Blade said.

"Not at all," Captain Yost replied. "The quest for the good life is good for all, and the good of the many outweighs the good of the few."

"Did you make that up?"

"No," Captain Yost said. "Every school child in Atlanta is taught about social values. That's a saying we memorize."

"So you . . . dispose of unproductive members of your society for the good of all the rest?" Blade inquired.

Captain Yost nodded. "Now you've got it."

"How do you determine who is productive and who isn't?"

"The Euthanasia Directorate determines the value of every person."

Blade gazed at the seven monoliths, edifices now imbued with a sinister aura. "What about the other Directorates?"

"The Civil Directorate codifies and administers our Civil Rights," Yost revealed. "The Ethics Directorate regulates morality and sex—"

"How do they regulate morality?" Blade interrupted.

"You know," Captain Yost said. "They insure one group doesn't try to force its morality on others."

"Give me an example."

"Back in the old days there were those who objected to sex between consenting adults of the same gender," Yost detailed. "But today, anything goes. The personal rights of sexual partners are protected by the Ethics Directorate."

"You place a lot of importance on your rights," Blade noted.

"Civil Rights are everything to a civilized society," Yost said. "Our rights define our freedom."

"I didn't think freedom required defining," Blade observed.

"If you'd attended our schools, you would understand," Captain Yost stated. He nodded at the monoliths. "The Community Directorate operates our mandatory daycare and schools. Abortions and birth control are under the jurisdiction of the Life Directorate. The Progress Directorate is devoted to science. And the Orientation Directorate makes sure everyone's head is on straight."

"They what?"

"They test everyone to guarantee each person has the right values," Captain Yost replied. "The right outlook on life."

"Who decides which values are the right ones?"

"The pyschologists at Orientation, of course."

"Of course," Blade said.

"Yes, sir," Captain Yost declared happily. "I'm very fortunate to be living here. You might consider doing the same."

"Outsiders are allowed to live in Atlanta?" Blade asked.

Captain Yost nodded. "After a three-month indoctrination course, you'd fit right in."

"Where would I take this course?"

"At Orientation. Actually, you'd live there the whole three months. When they got through with you, you'd be a new person."

"I bet I would," Blade concurred. The more he discovered, the more alarmed he became. The citizens of Atlanta were manipulated like puppets, brainwashed into accepting a social philosophy and compelled to live their lives subject to the Directorates. The seven heads of the Directorates, the Peers, wielded total power over the populace. He had encountered dictatorships before, but never a system like Atlanta's. The dictator wasn't a single person; the tyrant was a system of rights stipulated by a select few.

"One day, our government will serve as the model for the government of the world," Captain Yost boasted.

"You're kidding."

"Nope," Yost responded. "Other cities will naturally follow our example once the word gets around."

Blade almost laughed. *There* was a mind-boggling thought! "How did all of this come about?"

"I'm a bit rusty on my history," Captain Yost said. "But I know it started a few years after the war. The federal and state governments had collapsed. There was a shortage of food, clothing, and fuel. The people were desperate. That's when Dewey appeared."

"Who was he?"

"An intellectual. Before the war he was a professor at a university. He organized the survivors and wrote Atlanta's constitution. He was responsible for overseeing the construction of the wall to protect the citizens from the looters and the mutants." Captain Yost paused. "Dewey was the greatest man who ever lived."

"Did he set up the Directorates?" Blade probed.

"Yeah."

They were entering a commercial district. The pedestrian traffic was much heavier, and light vehicle traffic had materialized.

"There aren't a lot of cars and trucks on the road," Blade pointed out.

"Cars and trucks are a luxury very few can afford," Captain Yost said. "Most are operated by government employees."

"Do you manufacture everything the city needs?" Blade asked.

"Most of it," Yost disclosed. "We mint our money, grow most of our food, and produce the clothes on our backs. We've established trade relations with several other cities."

"Which ones?"

Captain Yost ignored the query. He turned left, heading along a narrow street.

Blade looked back. Glisson was walking between two of the troopers, his features downcast. The pedestrians all studiously minded their own business; not one gave the patrol any attention.

"So who are you searching for in Atlanta?" Captain Yost inquired.

"I was told that a cousin of mine, Llewellyn Snow, lives here," Blade lied. "I hoped I can find her."

"You don't know her address?"

"No," Blade said.

"The Central Directory in the Civil Directorate should be able to help you," Captain Yost commented. "Your Escort will assist you in using the Directory."

Blade heard the sound of an engine coming from above him and to the left. He glanced skyward and spotted another plane, a different model than the one the Warriors had seen previously. "Does Atlanta have an airport?"

"Sure does," Yost confirmed. "The Peers and other executive types use them on a regular basis."

"Where do they fly?"

"Oh, here and there."

Blade received the distinct impression the officer was being evasive when it came to the subject of possible trade and diplomatic contacts. Again, why? Was the information a secret?

The first monolith towered over the structures directly ahead. The seven Directorates were arranged in a line from north to south along a broad boulevard.

"That's the Community Directorate," Captain Yost

divulged. "Then comes Euthanasia and Civil."

Blade gazed at the nearest structure. People were coming and going through a half-dozen glass doors, bustling about their business. Ninety-eight percent of the citizens wore jumpsuits. The rest were either police or men and women in red suits. "Why does almost everyone wear jumpsuits?" he asked.

"For identification purposes," Captain Yost replied.

"How do you mean?"

"The practice was started after the war when there was a shortage of clothing," Yost detailed. "Each person was allotted a few uniforms and that was it. Dewey instituted the custom of having the uniforms color coded according to trade or profession. For instance, anyone wearing a brown uniform is in a manual-labor field. Green uniforms denote lower-level Admin types, like file clerks or accountants or secretaries. Light blue is for middle-management positions."

"What about the red suits?" Blade inquired.

"Upper echelon."

"How convenient," Blade remarked. "I even saw children wearing jumpsuits."

"Everyone must wear the color of their class," Captain Yost said. "It's illegal to do otherwise."

"The people don't mind?"

Yost seemed surprised by the question. "Why should they mind? Our system is logical and effective. Everyone knows their place, and there's a place for everyone."

They passed the first monolith, headed for the second.

"Give me a break, Yost," Glisson spoke up. "Why don't you let me go? I'll never return to Atlanta. My word on it."

Captain Yost laughed. "Do you think I'm an idiot? I wouldn't trust you as far as I could throw you."

"Please. Let me go."

"I can't," Captain Yost said. "You know that. You've made your bed. Now lie in it."

"I don't want to die!" Glisson cried.

"Everyone dies sooner or later," Captain Yost philosophized. "Death is inevitable."

"Can't you spare him?" Blade interjected.

Captain Yost shook his head. "I have my responsibility to the citizens of Atlanta. And the Civil Council has made it clear that social parasites must be eradicated."

Blade stared at the glass doors to the Euthanasia Directorate, not more than 40 yards off. What should he do? Allow the police to stick Glisson in a Sleeper Chamber? If he intervened on the hobo's behalf, what would the police do? Finding Llewellyn Snow was his main priority. Trying to rescue Glisson would only jeopardize his task and his life.

But what other choice did he have?

"How many travelers have you disposed of this way?" Blade queried, calculating the distance to the doors and studying his surroundings.

"I thought you understood," Captain Yost said. "We only dispose of bums like Glisson."

Blade looked at the officer and smiled. "Thank you."

Captain Yost paused. "For what?"

"For making my mind up for me," Blade said, and struck.

Chapter Eight

"Where the blazes are those cow chips?"

"What's a cow chip?"

Hickok glanced at Chastity. "Never you mind, missy." He faced the metropolis, surveying the highway. A stand of trees and brush obstructed his view of Blade. He'd seen his friend reach the road and head for the city, and he'd expected Rikki to intercept Blade before the giant had gone very far. But Blade had proceeded for hundreds of yards, with Hickok keeping his eyes glued to his sidekick every step of the way until the vegetation blocked his view. "Rikki should have caught up with Blade by now," he commented.

"He didn't," Chastity said.

"How do you know?"

"Because there's Blade," Chastity stated, pointing at the wall.

Hickok swiveled, recognizing, even at such a distance, Blade's unmistakable form near a gate. Figures in blue were visible. "Blast!"

"What's wrong?" Chastity inquired.

"Rikki was supposed to stop Blade," Hickok said. "What went wrong?"

"I don't know. What do we do now?"

The gunman looked at the child, then at the city. Blade was entering Atlanta, escorted by troopers!

"Do we stay here?" Chastity questioned.

"I need to chew this over a bit," Hickok said.

Chastity's forehead creased and she gazed at his hands. "I don't see any food."

"I didn't mean food."

"Do you have candy?" Chastity asked hopefully.

"Nope."

"Then what are you going to chew?"

Hickok sighed and patted her head. "You're lucky that you weren't born a cat."

"Why?"

"Never mind."

"Do you know something?" Chastity queried.

"What?"

"Sometimes you say the weirdest things."

"Hush," Hickok told her. "I'm tryin' to think." He scratched his chin and stroked his mustache, debating his options. His initial impulse was to go into Atlanta after Blade, but he would need to tote the girl, risking her capture or worse. He could stay put until Blade and Rikki returned, but he didn't cotton to the notion of twiddling his thumbs when his buddies might be in trouble. Or he could search for Rikki. He decided the third course was best. "Come on," he directed, rising.

Chastity stood. "Where are you taking me?"

"We need to find Rikki," Hickok said.

"Is he lost?"

"Either that or taking a nature break."

Chastity cocked her head to the left. "What's a nature break?"

"Never mind."

"You sure say that a lot."

"Walk right behind me," Hickok instructed her. "Be as quiet as you can."

"Like a little mouse?"

Hickok nodded, grinning. "Like a mouse." He slung Blade's M-16 over his right shoulder, insured the Uzi was snug under his left arm, and loosened the Pythons in their holsters.

"I can carry one of your guns," Chastity offered.

"No thanks."

"Aren't they heavy?"

"No."

"Then why can't I carry one?"

"Because I don't want you shootin' yourself in the foot," Hickok said.

"I won't shoot it. I promise."

"No."

"You're no fun," Chastity declared.

"My missus says the same thing." Hickok walked into the undergrowth, alert for anything out of the ordinary. Rikki's absence confounded him. The Family's supreme martial artist was capable of handling any foe, and taking Rikki unawares was next to impossible. So where the dickens was he?

"Where is your family?" Chastity inquired.

"Hush up."

"You're not being nice."

Hickok halted and looked back. "We can't make any noise, Chastity. There are a lot of bad things in the forest. We must be very careful."

Her eyes widened as he gazed at high weeds to the right. "Do you mean more icky things?"

Hickok nodded.

"I'll be quiet," Chastity promised.

The Warrior turned and resumed his hunt, his hands resting on his Colts. There wasn't a clear path in sight, and he had no way of knowing the exact direction Rikki had taken toward the highway. He skirted a tree and threaded through a cluster of bushes, constantly checking on Chastity. Her fright was transparent, and she repeatedly bumped into his legs as she tried to stick close to him.

Birds were chirping in a tree to the left.

Hickok became increasingly annoyed the farther they traveled. The forest had swallowed Rikki-Tikki-Tavi without a trace. He reached a clearing and stopped, his blue eyes narrowing as his gaze fixed on the great hole in the center.

"What's that?" Chastity whispered anxiously.

"A trap," Hickok answered, then advanced. He moved to the rim of the pit and examined the caved-in covering. Someone had done a dandy job of camouflaging the affair. With Rikki in a hurry to reach Blade, the martial artist might not have noticed until too late.

"Did Rikki fall in?"

"Maybe," Hickok replied, stepping around the pit, inspecting the ground. He found scuff marks on the far side and partial footprints leading to the east. The bottom of the pit did not contain spikes or stakes, and there was no evidence of blood. Rikki must still be alive!

"Hickok."

"Not now."

"It's important."

The gunman stared at the girl. "What could be so danged important?"

"I have to tinkle."

"What?"

"I have to tinkle."

"You have to go to the bathroom?"

Chastity nodded sheepishly.

"*Now*?"

"I'm sorry," Chastity said.

"Don't be sorry," Hickok declared. "When you have to go, you have to go. So go."

"Will you watch me?"

Hickok motioned at the trees. "A lady doesn't let a man watch her tinkle."

Chastity looked at the woods. "An icky thing could get me."

"I'll stand guard," Hickok offered. "You can go behind one of the trees."

"You won't let an icky thing get me?"

"I said I'd stand guard," Hickok reiterated, leading her to the trees to the south. "Now get to it."

Chastity nervously walked around the wide trunk of a lofty maple tree.

Hickok leaned against the trunk and impatiently waited for her to finish. He watched the tops of the trees rustle and saw a flock of sparrows winging to the west.

Several minutes elasped.

"Are you done?" Hickok demanded.

Chastity did not respond.

The Warrior straightened and turned. "Are you done, little one?"

"Yes," she replied, but whispering so softly the word was barely audible.

"Speak up," Hickok said.

"I can't," Chastity whispered.

"Why not?"

"The thing might get mad."

"What thing?" Hickok asked, hastening to her aid, taking four strides and freezing in midstep, his hands on his Pythons, his skin prickling. "Don't move!"

"I won't," Chastity said softly.

And well she shouldn't. The slightest move could cause the creature ten feet away to launch itself at her. The thing was a mutant, a hideous beast with a squat torso and long, thin arms and legs. Shaggy brown hair covered its form. An oversized head rested on sloping shoulders. Above a slit of a mouth and a flat nose were baleful black eyes, fixed on the girl.

Hickok had never seen anything like it. The creature somewhat resembled photographs of apes in the Family library, but he was at a loss to explain the presence of apes in Georgia—unless several had escaped a zoo or circus during the Big Blast and their progeny had survived. The thing vaguely reminded him of a chimpanzee, but a monstrous, deformed caricature of the breed.

The beast growled, its lips stretching to reveal nasty, tapered teeth.

Hickok," Chastity said, sounding extremely scared.

"Don't move!" Hickok advised.

But she did.

The creature growled again and took a lumbering pace forward, its arms reaching out.

Chastity screamed and bolted, dashing past the Warrior, fleeing into the clearing.

With a feral snarl, the mutant gave chase, astoundingly swift for such an ungainly animal. Relishing the prospect of a fresh meal, slavering at the mouth, the thing was not inclined to tolerate any interlopers.

Hickok's Pythons were sweeping free of their holsters when the mutant slammed into him.

Chapter Nine

"I won't ask twice," said the man with the red hair when Rikki balked at releasing his sword. "I saw how you took care of Big John and Dale, so I know you're skillful. One of the best I've ever seen. But you're no match for thirty-seven archers, and killing you would be a waste. Why don't you put your sword down and we'll talk?"

Rikki-Tikki-Tavi sighed, removed the scabbard from under his belt, and slowly placed the katana on the ground. He straightened, resigned to yet another delay. Resistance would be foolish.

The man with the red mustache and beard grinned. "That's better. I'm glad you have some common sense." He strolled toward the Warrior. "My name, by the way, is Locklin."

"I am Rikki."

Locklin stopped and extended his right hand. "I'm pleased to make your acquaintance."

Rikki shook. "Do you treat all your prisoners with such hospitality?"

"No," Locklin admitted. "But we don't often snare someone like you."

"Why am I special?" Rikki asked, releasing Locklin's hand, impressed by the man's firm handshake.

"Because we usually trap police or Terminators looking

for us," Locklin said. "Only once before have we caught someone who wasn't from Atlanta."

"And you're certain I'm not?"

"For several reasons," Locklin stated. "Anyone from Atlanta would be wearing a prescribed uniform. You're not. Citizens are not permitted to leave the city unless they obtain a special pass, and the Peers never issue such a pass. And finally, no one in Atlanta would be able to use their hands and feet like you do. What was that?"

"I'm somewhat proficient at the martial arts," Rikki answered. He nodded at the two forms sprawled on the turf. "I did not harm them. They will awaken shortly."

Locklin looked at several of his band. "Rouse them," he ordered. Then, to the rest, he made a twisting motion with his left hand and all the bows were lowered.

"Hand signals," Rikki remarked.

Locklin nodded. "They come in handy at times."

"You are the leader of these Freedom Fighters?" Rikki asked.

"That I am," Locklin confirmed. "I started the band fourteen years ago, in the heady days of my youth."

Rikki scanned the men and women. "Are all of them from Atlanta?"

"Yes," Locklin said. "Each and every one was a victim of persecution, or their family was. Each and every one has a score to settle with the Peers."

"Who are these Peers?"

Locklin pointed eastward. "Our camp is five miles off. Join us for a meal, and I'll tell you everything of importance about the Peers and Atlanta."

"I can't."

"Why not?" Locklin questioned.

"I am with two friends," Rikki said. "I won't leave without them."

"Where are they?"

Rikki watched three men engaged in awakening Big John and Dale. His instincts told him Locklin was trustworthy,

but he was not about to needlessly endanger Hickok and
Blade by exercising a premature confidence. He looked
at the rebel leader. "Sorry. I'm not at liberty to say."

Locklin shrugged. "A person can't be too trusting
nowadays. I won't press the issue." He paused. "I *will*
insist on your accompanying us to our camp. On my word
of honor, you will not be harmed."

"I will go with you," Rikki said. For the moment, he
was outnumbered and constrained to comply.

Big John was rising and rubbing his sore neck. His gaze
rested on the man in black and his face went crimson.
"You! You did this to me!" He clenched his fists and took
a step toward the Warrior.

Locklin moved between them. "John! No!"

Furious, Big John glared at the diminutive stranger. "He
hurt me!"

"He could have killed you," Locklin commented.

"I want to tear him apart," Big John declared.

"He is our guest," Locklin said. "I've given my word
that he will not be harmed."

Big John gaped at Locklin. "You can't be serious."

"Very."

The big man's hands relaxed and he frowned. "This isn't
fair. I want another crack at him."

"You heard me," Locklin said harshly.

"Yeah," Big John stated, pouting. "I heard."

Locklin glanced at the martial artist. "I want your word
that you will hear me out."

Rikki did not respond.

"Look, I know you'll try to escape the first chance you
get," Locklin said. "I'm no dummy. And I'm a shrewd
judge of character. If you give your word, I know you'll
keep it. So I want your word you'll listen to what I've got
to say. Do I have it?"

Rikki-Tikki-Tavi realized all eyes were upon him. If he
declined, Locklin would still demand he accompany them
to their camp, probably under close guard. If he accepted,

he might be able to name his own terms. "If I agree, I want your word in return."

"On what?"

"You will allow me to leave without interference," Rikki said.

"Is that all? You have it," Locklin vowed.

"Then I give my word I will hear you out."

Locklin beamed. He looked at Big John. "Give him his weapons."

"What?"

"Do you need your ears checked?" Locklin quipped. "Give the man his weapons."

Big John's features reflected utter bewilderment. "But, boss—"

"There are no buts about it," Locklin said testily. "Do it!"

With manifest reluctance, Big John retrieved the katana and the Uzi and gave them to the man in black.

"Thank you," Rikki said, taking his weapons.

Locklin stared at Dale. "And how are you doing?"

"I feel like I was flattened by a two-ton boulder," Dale replied. "But I can walk."

"Then we head out," Locklin commanded. He raised his right arm and gestured to the east. "To camp. Scarlet and Jane on point. Partington and Stutely, the rear. Move it, people."

The band mobilized rapidly, forming a column of twos, the rear guard and the point pair hurrying to their respective positions.

"Your band is highly trained," Rikki said, complimenting their leader.

Locklin smiled proudly. "They've worked hard. Our lives are on the line every day. If we don't stay on our toes, we're dead."

The Freedom Fighters marched to the east, Locklin and Rikki at the had of the column.

"Why bows?" Rikki asked after they had traversed a

mile.

Locklin chuckled. "It does seem an odd choice, doesn't it? Bows and arrows against guns and flamethrowers—"

"Flamethrowers?" Rikki asked, interrupting.

"The Terminators use flamethrowers," Locklin disclosed. "They can burn you to a crisp at three hundred feet."

Rikki thought of the words Chastity had used concerning her mother. The child had claimed the Bubbleheads burned her mom. "Are these Terminators known by other names?"

"Like what?"

"Bubbleheads."

Locklin did a double take, then laughed. "Where did you hear that? Bubbleheads is the word the children use to describe the Terminators."

"Unusual name," Rikki observed.

"Not really. The Terminators wear fireproof outfits, including oversized helmets. The headgear makes them look like beings from another planet."

"Or Bubbleheads," Rikki said.

Locklin grinned. "You've got it."

"And you fight them with bows?"

"Guns are a scarce commodity," Locklin explained. "We've appropriated a few, but obtaining ammunition is next to impossible. Bows are easier to locate or construct, and they're relatively silent."

"The odds would seem to be stacked against you," Rikki mentioned. "Forty against an entire city."

"Forty against the police and the Terminators," Locklin said, correcting the Warrior. "True, there are several hundred Storm Police and a score of Terminator squads. But justice is on our side. We'll triumph eventually."

"I know nothing of conditions inside Atlanta," Rikki said.

"Then allow me to fill you in," Locklin proposed. "Atlanta is ruled by seven people, five men and two women, known as Peers. They form a body called the Civil Council, and everyone in Atlanta is under their thumb. The city has become a police state. Liberty has died and been replaced by legalistic fascism.''

''Why do the residents tolerate such a situation?'' Rikki inquired. ''Why don't they revolt en masse?''

''You don't understand the first thing about revolutions,'' Locklin said. ''It's not as simplistic as that.''

''Enlighten me,'' Rikki prompted.

Locklin stared at a fluffy white cloud overhead. ''Study history. There have been countless oppressed societies. Dictators have come and gone. Fascists, Communists, and despots of every stripe have left their legacy of hatred and death. Millions, no, billions of men and women have lived under autocratic regimes. Most of them never revolted. Why? Because they accepted the status quo. They were indoctrinated into complacency. They valued having food on the table more than they valued their freedom.''

''Aren't you being a bit hard on them?'' Rikki inquired. ''Dictatorships invariably have powerful military machines to enforce governmental edicts.''

Locklin looked at the man in black. ''You know your history. Then you know about the American Revolution. The colonies threw off the British yoke because the majority of the colonists considered their freedom worth any price.'' He paused. ''When I was twelve, I found a shelf of ancient books in a library. The paper was yellow and threatened to crumple at the touch. One of the books was a history of the American Revolution, and I still feel a tingle every time I remember the words of Patrick Henry.''

Rikki's mind drifted back to his schooling days at the Home. ''What about Henry?''

''His words fired my soul,'' Locklin declared, and his eyes lit up as he quoted his favorite passage: ''I know not what course others may take; but for me, give me liberty, or give me death!''

Rikki recognized Locklin's sinerity; the rebel leader was

ardently devoted to his cause.

"I'd like to have those words engraved on my tomb-
stone," Locklin was saying. "A man couldn't have a finer
epitaph."

A flock of starlings abruptly winged from a stand of trees
75 yards ahead of the column.

Rikki casually unslung the Uzi and cradled the automatic
next to his waist. He scrutinized the trees, then glanced at
the pair on point. Scarlet and Jane were 30 yards off,
advancing cautiously, and they did not appear to be unduly
concerned about the starlings.

"People become conditioned to a way of life," Locklin
stated. "When you get down to the nitty-gritty, most people
don't want to rock the boat. They'd rather roll with the
flow."

A bush near the stand of trees quivered for a few seconds.
Scarlet and Jane did not notice.

Sliding his finger over the Uzi trigger, Rikki glanced at
Locklin. "We're walking into a ambush," he calmly
announced.

"I know," Locklin said, unruffled.

"You know?"

"Of course. Scarlet signaled me over a minute ago."

"I didn't see him signal you," Rikki said.

"When he scratched his nose with his left hand," Locklin
detailed. "I told you, hand signals are essential to our
operation."

"If you know the ambush is there," Rikki mentioned,
"why are we walking into it?"

Locklin smiled and slowly unslung his long bow. "You'll
see. When I give the word, flatten."

"Any idea who is in those trees?"

"It's probably a Storm Police patrol," Locklin replied.
"A dozen troopers with automatic rifles, M-16s and
AR-15s."

"And you're going to take them on with just bows?"
Rikki asked skeptically.

"Pay close attention," Locklin said. "You may learn something."

The two on point tramped eastward without betraying their knowledge of the ambushers, hardly paying any attention to the stand of trees. Scarlet, a lean man with brown hair, and Jane, a woman with sandy tresses, came abreast of the stand, then passed it.

Rikki evaluated the ambushers as professionals. Whoever was concealed in the brush was letting the point pair pass, waiting for the main column to get closer. A routine tactical ploy. He felt uncomfortable as he drew nearer, knowing a rifle sight might be trained on his body.

"Get ready," Locklin whispered.

The column reached a point approximately 20 yards from the stand. They were crossing a strip of high weeds.

Rikki detected a faint click.

"Now!" Locklin bellowed, and every Freedom Fighter dove for the dirt.

And not a split second too soon.

The metallic chatter of automatic gunfire erupted from the trees, creating an instant din as the ambushers all fired simultaneously. Four men in dark blue uniforms materialized, spraying the weeds ineffectually.

On their sides below the hail of gunfire, the Freedom Fighters were quickly notching arrows. They stayed down until the ambushers momentarily ceased firing for a lack of targets, and then half of the band sprang erect and loosened a volley of glimmering shafts while the remainder slid into the undergrowth and vanished.

Rikki popped up in time to see a pair of the men in blue fall, one screeching with an arrow through his throat, the second with a shaft jutting from his chest. The Warrior cut loose with an indiscriminate burst at the stand and was rewarded by the sight of a trooper pitching from the branch of a tree. He ducked low again as the ambushers resumed their withering fire. Around him the Freedom Fighters were doing likewise.

Locklin was smiling, actually enjoying himself. He looked at Rikki and winked.

The man in black could guess Locklin's strategy. The rest of the band was circling around the ambushers, coming at the troops from the rear. If the Freedom Fighters were adept at stealth, the battle would be over within a minute unless the ambushers had a surprise of their own.

They did.

Rikki saw Locklin's eyes widen as the rebel leader stared skyward, and the Warrior swiveled his gaze in the same direction. His abdominal muscles inadvertently tightened.

A plane was making a strafing run toward them!

Chapter Ten

Blade's plan, formulated on the spur of the moment, was elementary and direct: overpower the patrol, grab Glisson, and head for the hills or some semblance thereof. By taking the initiative when they were 35 yards from the Euthanasia Directorate, out in the open and not hemmed in, he maximized the advantage of his superior size and reach. His attack was totally unexpected. Captain Yost and two of the troopers were flattened by roundhouse haymakers before the trio still standing awoke to the fact they were under assault. The shortest of the three grabbed for the blackjack in its holster on his right hip, only to find himself toppling over after the giant delivered an excruciating kick to his testicles.

"Get him!" hissed the heaviest of the two patrolmen left. He whipped his blackjack from its holster and swung at the giant's chin, but failed to connect. The standard police blackjack was seven inches in length, consisting of a circular metal knob attached to a flexible handle, encased in brown leather. In the hands of an expert, the weapon could incapacitate or kill, and the trooper was adept at its use. He closed in, aiming another blow at the Warrior, foolishly expecting to end the fray quickly.

The second trooper drew his blackjack and waited for an opening.

With pantherish speed and grace, Blade side stepped the

policeman and used the edge of his right hand to crush his foe's throat. The man gagged and stumbled, his knees buckling, his arms waving wildly. Blade wrenched the blackjack free and turned to confront the final trooper.

Voicing an inarticulate cry of rage, the last policeman lunged.

Blade used his left forearm to block a descending swipe of the trooper's blackjack, then countered with a brutal smash to the man's nose. The cartilage crushed and blood spurted, and with a whine of despair the man threw himself backwards. Blade brought the blackjack up from his right knee, the metal ball smacking into the trooper's chin and crunching his teeth together.

The policeman tottered and went down.

Every pedestrian within 50 yards was immobile, watching the tableau in horrified astonishment.

Time to hit the road.

Blade glanced to the right and the left, and it was his turn to feel astonished as he saw that Glisson was gone. He glimpsed the tattered tramp hastening away to the east, weaving through the throng, and he sprinted in pursuit.

The transfixed citizens galvanized into frightened activity, scurrying from the giant's path.

Annoyed at Glisson's departure, Blade quickened his pace behind the hobo. From the direction of Glisson's travel, Blade deduced that the old-timer was heading for the gate they'd entered, possibly hoping to get out of Atlanta before being apprehended by another police patrol. Blade increased his pace again as he spotted Glisson's head and shoulders.

The oldster was moving at a spry clip. He looked over his left shoulder once, his face a mask of fear as he saw the giant. At the next intersection he took a left into a narrow street, sticking to the sidewalk.

Blade was gaining. The farther they went, the fewer people they encountered who had witnessed the fight with the police. Many of the amblers stared at him as he passed, but not one tried to interfere. He saw Glisson take a right and pounded after him. The old-timer was moving faster than Blade would have thought Glisson was capable of.

The pedestrians on the packed sidewalk were inadvertently slowing the Warrior, compelling him to proceed prudently to avoid a collision.

Glisson wasn't so careful.

The hobo looked back once more, and that act proved his undoing. He crashed into a woman in a brown jumpsuit and they both took a tumble.

Blade reached them before either could rise. He grabbed Glisson by the scruff of the collar and hauled the man erect.

"Let go of me!" Glisson snapped, thrashing.

"Calm down," Blade urged.

"Let go, damn you! I want to get out of here!"

"You don't stand a chance by yourself," Blade noted. "I can help you."

"Why should you help me?" Glisson demanded doubtfully.

"I dont' want to see an innocent person die," Blade said.

Glisson quit resisting. "Maybe we can help each other."

Blade released his grip. He noticed the woman on the sidewalk, gawking at them in amazement. "Are you okay?" he asked.

She nodded.

"Let me help you," Blade offered, extending his right hand.

She shook her head and stood, backpedaling before he could touch her. "No! I'm fine! Really!" She spun and fled into the crowd.

"The people here are sheep," Glisson remarked distastefully.

Blade took the old-timer's left arm and propelled him forward. "We must get out of Atlanta," he said.

Glisson snorted. "Tell me about it."

"You know the city much better than I do," Blade commented. "How can we escape? Over the wall?"

"Don't be an idiot," Glisson responded. "The outer wall

is twenty feet high and manned by armed guards."

"How else then?"

"We could bluff our way through one of the gates," Glisson proposed.

"Sounds risky to me," Blade said.

"And staying here isn't?" Glisson countered. "They're going to gas me in a Sleeper Chamber if I don't think of a way out."

Blade stared at the crowd, thinking. The police would be expecting them to try such a gambit, and the number of gate guards would likely be increased. Perhaps a wiser course would be to do something completely unforeseen, an act so off the wall that the authorities would never anticipate it. What would be the very last thing the police would expect?

"Do you have a better idea?" Glisson asked.

"Yes," Blade answered as inspiration dawned.

"What?"

"We go to the Civil Directorate."

Glisson halted so quickly, he almost tripped over his own feet. "What?"

"We were heading for the Civil Directorate, right?" Blade said. "Let's go there."

The old-timer's lips twitched as he studied the giant from head to toe. "Funny. You don't look like a congenital moron."

"I'm serious," Blade stressed.

"That's what scares me," Glisson said. "I'm trapped in Atlanta with an imbecile."

"Listen to me. Where is the last place they would expect us to go?"

"To the nearest Storm Police station to give ourselves up," Glisson replied.

"They would never expect us to go to the Civil Directorate," Blade stated. "They'll be on our trail, and they'll be searching everywhere except there."

"What makes you so sure?"

"Would you expect us to go to the Civil Directorate if you were them?" Blade inquired.

"No," Glisson admitted. "I'd credit us with more intelligence than that."

"Let me ask you a question," Blade said. "You've been here many times. When the police took you to the Visitors Bureau at the Civil Directorate, did they take you inside?"

"No," Glisson answered. "They always took me right up to the door, then took off. So what?"

"So if we show up at the Civil Directorate, requesting the services of an Escort, we won't be arousing any suspicion," Blade said.

"What if we're spotted by a patrol?"

"We could be spotted any time," Blade noted. "It's a risk we'll have to take."

"And why bother to ask for an Escort?" Glisson queried.

"I still need to find someone."

"Even with the Storm Police on our tail?"

Blade nodded. "So what do you say? Are you with me?"

"What choice do I have?" Glisson retorted.

"Can you get us to the Civil Directorate without using the main streets?" Blade asked.

Glisson grinned. "I know this part of the city well. I can do it."

"Then let's go," Blade announced.

The old-timer resumed walking. "I knew I shouldn't have come back here," he mumbled.

"Then why did you?"

"I haven't eaten a square meal in a week," Glisson said. "I'm too old for the life on the road. Scrounging up food and other necessities is harder every year." He paused. "In the past, I could count on two days of squares and a new set of threads if I came to Atlanta. I didn't know the damn Peers had changed their indigent policy."

"Why do you live on the road? Why don't you settle down?" Blade suggested.

"You can't teach an old dog new tricks," Glisson

responded with a smile. "I've lived on the road since I was knee high to a grasshopper."

"Isn't it dangerous, what with all the mutants and scavengers?"

"Yeah, it's dangerous," Glisson replied. "But the danger is part of the allure. When you're on the road, you never know what's over the next hill or around the next curve. Every day brings something new, something different." He paused and chuckled. "And my elephant gun does an excellent job of dissuading the mutants and scavengers."

"You have an elephant gun?"

"An old Marlin 45-70. Ammo is scarce, but when it comes to stopping power, there isn't a gun like it," Glisson said with pride.

"Where is your 45-70?" Blade asked.

"I hid it in a waterproof sack near the road about three-quarters of a mile from the city wall," Glisson detailed. "I don't want these pricks to confiscate it on some pretext."

Blade followed the old-timer into an alley. Glisson conducted him on a circuitous route down little-used streets. "We should find jumpsuits to wear," the Warrior mentioned after ten minutes.

Glisson glanced at the giant. "I can rustle one up for me, but they don't make jumpsuits your size. King Kong doesn't live here."

"King Kong?"

"I'll explain later."

They approached the third monolith from the west, emerging from an alley onto a street swarming with pedestrian and vehicle traffic.

"This was once called Spring Street," Glisson remarked. "Now it's known as Civil Street." He pointed to the southeast. "The road we came into Atlanta on was Constitution Boulevard." He nodded at the stretch of land occupied by the seven monoliths. "This was the State Capitol area before the war. Do you see that expressway on the far side of the Directorates?"

Blade nodded.

"Well, just beyond it a great American was buried," Glisson revealed. "He was a black man who tried to improve the social conditions for his race. Martin Luther King, Jr. Do you know what his gravesite is now?"

"No," Blade said.

"A city dump." Glisson sighed sadly. "All the old ways are gone with the wind. The Peers don't want the people of Atlanta to be aware of prewar conditions, to realize the freedom Americans once enjoyed. Hell. They've even altered the textbooks the kids study in school. I saw one once. It was pitiful. This one went on and on about the official doctrine of the Peers, something called humanism."

"It figures," Blade commented.

"We can cross there," Glisson said, indicating a nearby intersection.

They walked to the corner and waited with about ten others for a traffic light to change.

"Look," Glisson whispered, staring at the curb on the opposite side of the street.

Blade gazed in that direction and discovered a Storm Policeman who was also waiting to cross. They would pass each other on the crosswalk.

"He'll spot us for sure," Glisson said nervously.

"We can't turn back now," Blade responded.

"He'll blow the whistle on us."

The light had not changed yet.

"It's only been twenty minutes or so since we made our break," Blade noted. "I doubt they've had the time to spread our descriptions to every trooper in the city."

"I hope you're right," Glisson said.

The light changed and a WALK sign lit up."

"Let's go," Blade stated. "And try not to act jittery."

"Tell that to my bladder."

The groups of pedestrians on the curbs started across the street.

Blade stepped from the curb, his head held high, projecting a carefree air, purposely refraining from staring at the Storm Policeman. He held the blackjack in his right hand, tucked against his fatigue pants.

The trooper was coming straight at them.

Blade pretended to scan the far sidewalk, his eyes flicking over the Storm Policeman and assessing the man's disposition. The trooper appeared to be wrapped up in his own thoughts, oblivious to those around him.

They were ten feet apart.

Glisson bumped into the Warrior's left arm. He had scooted to Blade's left side to partially screen himself with the giant's body, and he was walking as close to Blade as he could get.

They were seven feet apart.

The Storm Policeman looked up and noticed the Warrior. His brown eyes narrowed as he examined Blade's features, and then he shifted his gaze to Glisson.

Five feet apart.

If the pores on Blade's skin had been large enough, Glisson would have crawled inside. He saw the trooper halt, and he gripped Blade's arm in desperation.

Blade felt the tramp's fingernails digging into his skin. He disregarded the pain and looked at the trooper.

Just as the Storm Policeman motioned with his right arm. "Hey, you!"

Chapter Eleven

Hickok's breath whooshed from his lungs as the incredibly powerful creature plowed into him, wrapped its spidery arms about his chest, and bore him to the hard ground. Putrid breath assailed the gunman's nostrils, and beady, malevolent eyes glared into his.

"Hickok!" Chastity screamed, checking her flight and whirling.

"Run!" the gunfighter bellowed, squirming in the mutant's grasp. His arms were pinned to his sides and he couldn't raise his Pythons.

The beast snarled and bared his fangs.

"Eat this, sucker!" Hickok declared, and angled the Colt barrels inward until they were flush with the creature's ribs. He squeezed both triggers.

Muffled by the mutant's hair and flesh, the Pythons blasted, their twin slugs penetrating the beast and searing the creature with overwhelming agony. It relinquished its hold and rolled to the left, roaring mightily.

Hickok rose to his knees, ready to add more shots if necessary, but the thing was still rolling. Suddenly it leaped up and darted into the undergrowth.

"Hickok!" Chastity cried.

"Stay put!" Hickok ordered, slowly standing. Where the dickens did the brute go? He backed toward the girl, surveying the vegetation. A puddle of red liquid drew his attention. Blood. The creature was undeniably hurt, seriously injured. Would the genetic deviate go off to lick its wounds, or would it hover and await an opportunity to pounce?

"There!" Chastity shouted.

"Where?" the Warrior asked, glancing at her.

"There," she repeated, pointing to their right. "I saw something move."

Hickok scrutinized the wall of vegetation enclosing the clearing. "I don't see anything."

"I saw it," Chastity insisted.

The gunman edged to the pit rim, Chastity by his right side.

"What do we do?" she inquired.

"We stay here for the time being."

"Why?"

"That critter can't take us by surprise here," Hickok informed her. "We'll sit tight and see if it skedaddles."

"Skedaddles? Is that bad or good?"

"We'll sit tight and see if it leaves," Hickok clarified.

From the forest to their right, concealed in the prolific greenery, the mutant growled.

"I'm scared," Chastity said.

"I won't let it get you," Hickok promised.

Chastity hugged his right leg. "Think there could be more?"

The gunman pursed his lips. He hadn't given the matter any brainwork. "I don't think so," he said to assure her.

Another growl punctuated his statement.

"Do you think it got Rikki?" Chastity inquired.

"I doubt it," Hickok replied. "Mutants don't like stringy meat."

"Is that a joke?"

"Keep quiet," Hickok directed her.

There was the crackle of brush and the rustling of leaves as the creature moved about, changing position.

"What's it doing?" Chastity asked.

"I don't know," Hickok confessed, trying to come up

with a solution to their dilemma. He didn't like the idea of being stuck in the clearing when Blade and Rikki needed his help. But if he tried to lead Chastity through the forest, the beast would undoubtedly attack. A ruse was called for, a foxy scheme to outwit the critter.

But what?

"Maybe we can hide in the hole?" Chastity suggested.

"Don't be . . ." Hickok said, starting to admonish her. Then he cut himself off, looking into the pit.

Hold the fort.

The pit was ten feet deep, circular, with sheer sides to prevent any hapless captive from clambering to freedom. Which was all well and good. But how did those doing the capturing haul their prisoners from the hole? Did they use a rope? Not likely, because the nearest tree capable of supporting a long, sturdy rope was 20 yards off. They would need to lug a lot of rope with them and assist their captive in exiting the trap.

No.

There had to be another way.

The gunfighter edged around the rim, his keen eyes inspecting the vegetation at the perimeter of the clearing.

Chastity hung onto his leg and shuffled with him.

"You can leave go of me," Hickok said softly.

"No way."

"I'm not going anywhere."

"No."

"I can't walk with you clingin' to me," Hickok observed.

"I won't let go," Chastity declared.

"Suit yourself," Hickok said. "But if that varmint comes after us again, I can't fight it very well with you slowin' me down."

Chastity stared up at him, indecision etched on her countenance.

"And there's something else you'd best keep in mind," Hickok told her.

"What?"

"If I tinkle my pants, it'll run all over your hands."

Chastity released his leg and scrunched up her nose.
"You wouldn't tinkle your pants," she said.

"I certainly hope not," Hickok stated. "My missus
would clobber me." He stepped nearer to the foliage on
the far side. Maybe he was wrong. Maybe the . . .

There it was.

The gunman hurried to the weeds bordering the clearing,
Chastity in tow. He grinned as he knelt next to an 11-foot
pole the thickness of his arm.

"What's that?" Chastity queried.

"Have you ever played hide and seek?"

Chastity nodded. "Lots and lots of time. Why?"

"We're going to play it again," Hickok said, holstering
his left Colt. He grabbed one end of the pole and dragged
it to the pit, then knelt and slid the end he'd held to the
bottom of the hole, slanting the shaft so over two feet
protruded above the lip.

"I don't get it," Chastity commented.

"You will." Hickok unslung the Uzi and placed the
weapon on the ground near the pole.

"What are you doing?"

"Hush." Next, Hickok slid his right Python into its
holster and unslung the M-16. After insuring the magazine
was loaded and flipping off the safety, he turned to the girl.
"Climb on my back."

"Why?"

The gunman sighed. "It's nice to know that women start
at an early age."

"Start what?"

"Never mind."

"There you go again."

"Just get on my back," Hickok instructed her, his eyes
raking the forest.

Chastity complied, locking her arms around his neck and
clamping her legs on his sides.

"Now hold on tight," Hickok cautioned. "I'm going to
slide down this pole to the bottom of the pit."

Chastity's grip tightened. "It's dark down there. The monster will get us."

"No," Hickok said. "We're going to give the monster a big surprise. Trust me."

"I trust you."

"Don't fret. It'll be a piece of cake," Hickok assured her. He surveyed the foliage, hoping the mutant wasn't watching, and gripped the pole with his left hand, looped his right through the carrying strap of the M-16, and slowly lowered into the pit, descending hand over hand to the dirt floor. Branches and grass mats littered the hole. He crouched and deposited Chastity.

"I don't like this," she mentioned.

"Think of it as hide and seek," Hickok said. "We're hiding from the mutant. If it finds us, it wins the prize."

"What prize?"

"A face full of lead," Hickok replied. He gripped the M-16 in both hands and settled on his knees. "Sit."

Chastity obeyed.

"Now we wait," the Warrior whispered. "We can't make a peep or the monster will hear us."

"I'll be quiet," Chastity promised.

Hickok stared at the top of the pole, resigned to a lengthy vigil if necessary. He cocked his head as gunfire erupted far off.

"Hickok?" Chastity said quietly.

"I knew it," the gunman muttered. "What?"

"Would you be my new daddy?"

For one of the few times in his entire life, the gunfighter was speechless. He glanced at the girl, stunned by the unexpected query.

"Would you? I need one."

Hickok didn't know what to say. "I already have a son," he blurted out.

"Ringo," Chastity said. "I know. Would you like a girl too?" She gazed at him earnestly, expectantly.

The gunman tore his eyes from her and looked at the pit

rim. "You should stay with kinfolk," he said huskily.

"Who are the Kinfolks? Relatives of yours?"

"No," Hickok responded. "I meant that you should stay with relatives of yours."

"I don't have any."

"Yes, you do. Your father's sister, remember? Your aunt. Blade is in Atlanta searching for her right now," Hickok told her.

Chastity frowned. "Oh."

"Something wrong?"

"I don't like her," Chastity declared. "I don't want to live with her."

"You should live with relatives," Hickok reiterated.

Chastity glumly stared at the floor. "I get it. You don't want to be my daddy."

The corners of the gunman's mouth curled downward. "It's not that. I have a son—"

"And you only want one child," Chastity said.

"It's not that—"

"Your wife would be upset," Chastity stated.

"Will you stop interruptin' me!" Hickok snapped. "I never said we only wanted one kid. As for my missus, I'm the head honcho in our marriage."

"The what?"

"I'm the boss," Hickok explained.

"You are?"

"Well, sort of. We divide the responsibility and the decisions fifty-fifty," Hickok elaborated.

"Even-Steven?"

"Well, not quite." Hickok reflected a moment. "Actually, although I'd never admit it to anyone else, my missus is the brains in our marriage."

"Would she like to have a little girl?" Chastity asked eagerly.

"She's always gripin' about being outnumbered," Hickok mentioned. He looked into her eyes. "But takin' on a new mouth to feed is a major decision. Sherry and I would have to talk it out, and Ringo should be prepared."

"Do you mean you'll think about it?" Chastity inquired with a hopeful lilt.

"I'll cogitate on it," Hickok said.

"You'll what?"

"I'll think about it."

"Yippee!" Chastity exclaimed, jumping up and hugging him.

The Warrior felt like he was being choked to death. "Whoa there, princess. Calm down. We've got to be quiet."

But it was too late.

Hickok's blood chilled as he heard a guttural snarl from overhead, and he craned his neck for a view of the rim. A savage visage glowered at him. The mutant was at the very edge next to the pole, holding the Uzi in its hairy left hand. As the gunman had contrived, curiosity had prompted the beast to emerge from cover and shuffle to the weapon lying near the pit. Hickok guessed that the mutant had picked up the automatic a second before Chastity yelled, and now it knew they were there. "Look out!" he shouted, shoving the girl aside and elevating the M-16.

With a bellow of bloodlust, the creature leaped into the pit.

Chapter Twelve

The white plane's twin-engines whined as the aircraft arced at the band of Freedom Fighters.

"Cover!" Locklin called out.

Rikki-Tikki-Tavi knew he would court certain death if he stood; the Storm Police in the stand of trees would mow him down before he covered a yard. On the other hand, lying in the weeds exposed him to the diving plane. He compromised. Clutching the Uzi in his left hand, he quickly scrambled on his hands and knees into the dense brush. Above him the sky was rent by the rattle of a large-caliber machine gun.

Someone screamed in torment.

The Warrior rolled to a squatting posture, finding Locklin and other men and women in green near him. Three of the band had not been as fortunate, and their prone forms were visible sprawled in the weeds.

"Tuck!" Locklin cried.

Rikki peered upward at the aircraft as the plane climbed for a second run.

A squat, bearded man, hunched over at the waist, hastened to Locklin. He held a crossbow in his muscular right hand. "Yes?"

"You know what to do," Locklin said.

Tuck nodded and knelt, reaching for a small, brown

leather pouch attached to his belt on his left hip. He opened the flap and extracted an unusually large arrowhead.

"That plane is history," Locklin declared.

A crossbow against an aircraft? Rikki watched as Tuck shifted and revealed a quiver of crossbow bolts suspended from his belt on his right side. "You must be an outstanding archer," Rikki commented.

Tuck looked at the man in black. "Have you ever seen this done before?" He placed the black crossbow on the grass.

"I've never seen anyone shoot down a plane with an arrow."

"Watch," Tuck said. He extracted a bolt from the quiver, a short, green arrow lacking a tip. The end of the shaft was hollow. "These were all the rage before the war," Tuck commented. "It's easy to use different arrowheads this way." He quickly inserted the threaded base of the over-sized arrowhead into the hollow end of the bolt and screwed the arrowhead tight.

"We possess such arrows where I come from," Rikki mentioned. "And I have a friend who is an excellent bowman. His name is Teucer. But I doubt even he could down a plane with a simple shaft."

"Not so simple," Tuck said, holding the bolt out for Rikki to examine. "This is an explosive arrowhead, and it's designed to detonate on impact."

"Where did you obtain it?"

"We found an abandoned house in Redan. In the basement was a cache of weapons," Tuck divulged. "The place must have belonged to a survivalist."

"The plane is coming in for another run," Locklin interjected.

Tuck scooped up his crossbow and stood. "Hold this," he said, handing the bolt to Rikki. He extended a metal stirrup from under the front of the bow, then rested the stirrup on the turf and slid his right boot into it to act as a brace and keep the bow in position while he pulled on the string. Using both hands, he gripped the string and pulled until there was a loud click. "The arrow," Tuck said, and Rikki returned the bolt.

"Hurry," Locklin ordered.

Tuck slid the bolt into a groove, aligning the shaft snugly. "I'm ready," he announced.

Rikki peered skyward through the brush and spotted the aircraft banking in from the west. He glanced at the stand of trees, expecting to see a Storm Policeman or two, but instead he spied several men and women in green. The other half of Locklin's band had circled and silently slain the remaining Storm Police.

Tuck was heading from cover, holding the crossbow with the stock pressed against his right shoulder.

Rikki followed for a better view.

"Stay hidden," Locklin warned him.

Tuck crouched behind a bush, his gaze fixed on the plane.

The white aircraft was swooping low over the landscape, over the section of ground the Freedom Fighters had vacated.

Rikki could imagine the pilot and gunners scanning the terrain for the band. The green attire worn by the Freedom Fighters would be extremely difficult to see from the air.

Tuck was tracking the plane's path with the crossbow.

"He's the best man we have with a crossbow," Locklin remarked from the Warrior's right elbow.

The aircraft wasn't more than 50 feet above tree level and 30 yards to the west when Tuck suddenly rose and sighted. He squeezed the trigger almost immediately, and the shaft was a blur as it sped to meet the plane.

"Hit the dirt!" Locklin yelled.

Rikki-Tikki-Tavi flattened as the forest rocked to a tremendous explosion. The aircraft was enveloped in a fiery ball, and the concussion snapped limbs from the tops of those trees nearest the blast. Debris flew in every direction, and a moment later the bulk of the plane, now a tangled, twisted, flaming mass of wreckage, plummeted to the field below with a resounding crash.

The Freedom Fighters voiced a collective cheer.

"We did it!" Locklin exclaimed happily, rising.

Rikki stood and regarded the black smoke billowing on the wind.

"That's the third plane we've shot down this year," Locklin boasted.

Big John and Dale were leading the other half of the band to rejoin Locklin.

"How did it go?" the rebel leader asked as they approached.

"No problem," Big John said. "We didn't lose anyone. They weren't expecting us to jump them from behind."

"How many did you bag?" Locklin inquired.

"Eight," Big John replied. "Four more were already dead."

"Should we collect their weapons?" Dale queried.

"Of course," Locklin directed.

Dale selected a half-dozen band members and they hurried off.

"Did you hear that?" Locklin asked the Warrior. "We took down another Storm Police patrol. Twelve more bastards bite the dust."

"You sound glad," Rikki noted.

"Why shouldn't I be?" Locklin retorted. "The Storm Police are our enemies."

"The Storm Police are pawns," Rikki stated. "If all that you have told me is true, your real enemies are the Peers."

"Yeah. But the Storm Police are the enforcement arm of the Civil Council," Locklin said.

"The Peers direct the Storm Police," Rikki mentioned. "The Peers are the ones manipulating the people of Atlanta. The Peers, in a literal sense, are the brains behind the operation."

"So?" Locklin responded. "What's your point?"

Rikki stared at the blazing aircraft. "So for fourteen years you have been resisting the Peers by harassing the patrols they send outside the wall. For fourteen years you have killed pawn after pawn, downed a plane now and then, and prided yourselves on your great victories. But you've been deluding yourselves.''

The Freedom Fighters were listening to his every word.

"You think so, eh?" Locklin said.

"I know so," Rikki declared emphatically. He looked at the rebel leader. "Do you play chess?"

"I can play chess," Locklin answered.

"Then you must be able to see the inconsistency in your strategy," Rikki expounded. "A person does not win a chess match by concentrating exclusively on an opponent's pawns. Taking pawns is not the point of the game, nor is taking pawns the point of your revolution. If you want to win a chess match, you must checkmate the king. If you want to win your revolution, if you want to free the people of Atlanta, you must checkmate the Peers.''

"He makes sense," one of the band commented.

"Have you ever tried to assassinate the Peers?" Rikki asked Locklin.

The rebel leader sheepishly averted his eyes. "No," he said softly.

"How else do you expect to win your revolution?" Rikki inquired. "You can wipe out Storm Trooper patrols for years to come, and I doubt the Peers will consider your band as much more than a petty annoyance. You may actually help them consolidate their power by giving them a threat they can arouse the populace against.''

Locklin studied the martial artist for a second. "I've never thought of our rebellion in quite that light. How is it you know so much about revolutions?"

"I'm a Warrior," Rikki revealed. "I am one of the select few who were chosen to protect my people from any and all threats. Warriors are required to take many classes in the art and psychology of warfare. We're trained to develop the capacity for creative thinking. My logic is elementary.''

"I agree with everything you've said," Locklin stated. "But it's easier said than done. Killing the Peers would be next to impossible.''

"But not impossible?"

Locklin's forehead creased and the shadow of a smile touched his lips. "No," he replied slowly. "Not utterly impossible."

Rikki gazed at the three dead Freedom Fighters. "Would you mind some advice from an outsider?"

"Not at all."

"If you want to resolve this conflict once and for all, if you want to end the persecution and restore freedom, if you want to insure future generations will not live under the yoke of tyranny, then you must eliminate the Peers and establish a new government. Unless those responsible for formulating and spreading totalitarianism are eradicated, no one can ever be truly free."

"Will you help us?" Locklin asked bluntly.

"I did not come here to fight a revolution."

"I don't care why you came here," Locklin said. "The fact is, you're here, and now you have a decision to make. Will you aid us in overthrowing the Peers, or will you stand idly by and do nothing?" He paused. "Somehow, I can't see you as the type to stand by and allow hundreds of thousands of innocent people to suffer."

Rikki-Tikki-Tavi gazed to the west.

"There is one chance in a million we can pull it off," Locklin went on, striving to convince this sagacious stranger. "Once a week the Peers meet in the Civil Directorate for an executive session of the Civil Council. It's the only time we can get them all under one roof with any certainty. They meet every week without fail." He grinned. "And guess what? They meet tomorrow night."

Rikki placed his left hand on the hilt of his katana.

"If you led us, we might be able to do it."

The Warrior glanced at the rebel leader. "You are the head of this band. I cannot lead your Freedom Fighters."

"Why not?"

"There could be repercussions," Rikki said.

"What kind of repercussions?" Locklin queried.

"Repercussions against my Family," Rikki replied. "Ordinarily, we do not meddle in the affairs of others unless they pose a threat to our existence. If I led your mission, I would be violating the cardinal rule of noninterference established by the Elders.''

"Can't you make an exception in our case?''

Rikki contemplated a moment. "On the other hand, my Family is now a member of the Freedom Federation, and the Federation is devoted to restoring liberty to the land.''

"What's the Freedom Federation? I've never heard of it,'' Locklin said.

"There are seven factions banded together in a mutual self-defense pact,'' Rikki explained.

"Would they help us fight the Peers?''

"They might,'' Rikki answered. "But I honestly can't guarantee they would.''

Locklin ran his left hand through his hair. "In any event, we're not waiting to find out. Tomorrow night the Civil Council meets. Tomorrow night we will put an end to their evil, or we will perish in the attempt. Are you with us or not?''

Rikki-Tikki-Tavi was a long time in responding. When he did, his mouth was curled wryly. "I'll tell you what. I must go into Atlanta to find a friend of mine—''

"One of those you mentioned earlier?'' Locklin said, interrupting.

"Precisely,'' Rikki said.

"Why is he in Atlanta?''

"He's looking for a relative of a young girl we found,'' Rikki elaborated. "Her parents were killed. She blamed her father's death on the Peers, and she told us her mother was slain by the Bubbleheads.''

"Does this girl have a name?''

"Chastity Snow.''

Locklin exchanged glances with several of his band.

"Do you know her?'' Rikki asked.

"I know of her,'' Locklin replied. "Rather, I know of her father. His name was Richard Snow, and he was the publisher of *The Atlanta Tribune*.''

"Why would the Peers have killed him?''

Locklin shook his head. "Beats me. All a person has to do is cross them once, and the Peers make sure they are never crossed again."

"Would the Peers eliminate a whole family because one member aroused their wrath?"

"If the Peers were angry enough, they'd eliminate the entire Snow family tree," Locklin stated. "Sons, daughters, cousins, in-laws, you name it. The Peers are ruthless."

Rikki's expression became thoughtful. "So if my friend starts asking questions about Chastity's relative, he could wind up in trouble?"

"He could wind up dead."

The Warrior faced in the direction of the metropolis. "Then I must enter Atlanta as quickly as possible. Every moment of delay increases the danger to my friend."

"You mentioned two friends," Locklin reminded the man in black.

"My second friend is with Chastity Snow," Rikki disclosed. "We must inform him of our plans."

Locklin smiled. "Then you're going in with us?"

"Technically, I won't lead you," Rikki said. "But I must go into the city anyway. And if your band wants to tag along, I would have no objection."

Locklin chuckled. "I like the way your mind works. Let's find your friend with Chastity and go kick ass. Where are they anyway?"

From perhaps a mile away, maybe less, came the blast of gunshots.

"I think I know," Rikki stated.

Chapter Thirteen

Blade's grip on the blackjack tightened as the Storm Policeman stepped up to them. The trooper was staring intently at the hobo.

"Hey! Glisson! It is you, isn't it?" the policeman asked.

Blade nudged the old-timer with his elbow.

"Yeah, it's me," Glisson answered in a fearful tone.

"Don't you remember me?" the trooper inquired. "Corporal Schwartz? I conducted you to the Civil Directorate about seven or eight years ago. Remember?"

Glisson studied the trooper's features, then beamed. "Sure. I remember you. You were the young private who was asking me a lot of questions about life on the road."

Corporal Schwartz grinned. "I always was the curious sort." He glanced at the light. "I'd better cross before the light changes."

"Nice seeing you," Glisson said.

Corporal Schwartz took a stride, then stopped. "Where's your Escort?"

Blade quickly nodded at the far curb. "Already crossed."

"Oh." Schwartz began to turn, to look at the opposite curb, when the light changed. He hesitated for a second, smiled, and hastened on his way.

Blade hurried to the sidewalk with Glisson right behind him.

"That was too damn close!" the hobo declared once they were safely on the curb.

"Didn't you know you're famous?" Blade quipped.

"Very funny," Glisson snapped.

"Lead on," Blade instructed. "We'd better reach the Visitors Bureau before another of your fans spots us."

"Smart-ass son of a bitch," Glisson mumbled.

"Let's go," Blade said impatiently.

They strolled toward a row of glass doors at the base of the Civil Directorate, mingling with a constant stream of humanity flowing into and exiting the structure.

"The Visitors Bureau is on the ground floor," Glisson informed the giant. "We go in those doors and hang a right."

"Do the Storm Police frisk everyone who enters the Direcorate?" Blade asked, thinking of the blackjack in his right hand.

"No. Why should they?" Glisson responded. "There's never any trouble inside the wall. The rebels only hit patrols on the outside."

"Play it cool once we're inside," Blade advised.

"Joe Cool, that's me," Glisson said.

Blade was both perplexed by, and grateful for, the manifest lack of interest the citizens of Atlanta displayed in Glisson and himself. They all seemed to be too wrapped up in their own lives to care about a pair of strangers. He attributed their attitude to the hectic lifestyle prevalent in the metropolis; the people were constantly on the go. Aside from a few cursory stares engendered by his exceptional size and physique, the residents of the city ignored him.

Glisson slowed as he approached the glass doors, dragging his heels apprehensively.

"Keep going," Blade commanded.

"Maybe we should reconsider," Glisson commented. "We could be asking for grief."

"We see this through," Blade stated. "I have someone to find."

"We could try and find this person by ourselves,"
Glisson proposed.

"In a muncipality this big?" Blade retorted skeptically.
"It would take years."

Glisson frowned and walked to the glass doors, hesitating
briefly before yanking on the handle and stepping inside.

Blade followed, feeling a degree of comfort in the sea
of citizens busily hurrying to and fro. A huge lobby fronted
the glass doors, crammed with people. On the opposite wall
were five elevators, all in use. Underfoot was a plush green
carpet.

"This way," Glisson declared, turning to the right. After
40 feet they came to an amply lit corridor containing an
apparently endless succession of office doors.

"Which one?" Blade queried.

The tramp marched over to a closed door on the right.
"This is it."

In large black letters on the door were the words
"VISITORS BUREAU: Open 24 Hours."

"They're open twenty-four hours a day?" Blade queried.

"Atlanta never shuts down," Glisson said. "Many of
the people are assigned to shift work." He opened the door
and went in.

A wooden counter ran the width of the room within two
yards of the door. Handling paperwork or fielding questions
behind it were six employees. Another four pencil-pushers
were at desks beyond the counter.

"May I help you?" offered an attractive woman in a
smart yellow dress. Pinned to the fabric below her right
shoulder was a small gold and white badge with a single
word imprinted on the plastic: "ESCORT."

Glisson sauntered to the counter. "You sure can, sweet
lips."

The woman took instant umbrage, her thin nose crinkling
distastefully, her mouth twisting downward for a second
until she caught herself and forced a mechanical smile on
her lips. "Tolerance for all, sir, is a virtue," she said
pleasantly. Her alert brown eyes matched her complexion,

and her curly hair formed an oval cap to her heart shaped face.

"Where'd you get that from, sister?" Glisson asked. "A fortune cookie?"

The woman glanced over the hobo's head at the giant in the leather vest and fatigue pants. "Are you with this gentleman, sir?"

"Unfortunately," Blade replied, and saw her grin. "And calling him a gentleman is stretching the limits of reality."

She burst into laughter.

"There's no need to be insulting," Glisson said angrily.

"My name is Eleanor," the woman disclosed in a professional manner. "I am here to . . ." she began. Then she abruptly stopped, examining the tramp's features. "Haven't you been here before, a long time ago?"

"I've been here gobs of times, you pretty thing," Glisson answered.

"I'll have to ask you to behave yourself," Eleanor cautioned.

"And if I don't?" Glisson baited her.

"Please," Eleanor said. "As a personal favor for me?"

Glisson leaned on the counter and leered at her. "What do I get if I'm a good little boy?"

The sound of Blade's right hand landing on the hobo's back in a transparently friendly gesture produced a distinct smack.

Glisson straightened and looked at the Warrior, his eyes widening.

"If you're a good little boy," Blade stated mockingly, "you get to keep your teeth. Does that sound fair to you?"

Eleanor's eyes were twinkling.

"I was just having some fun," Glisson protested.

"Have you forgotten the reason we're here?" Blade inquired.

"Why are you here?" Eleanor asked.

"I'm searching for a relative of mine," Blade told her. "An officer informed me that you could find her using something called the Central Directory."

Eleanor nodded. "The Central Directory is a listing of the name, address, identification number, medical record, and personal history of every citizen in Altanta. We access the information through our computer."

"You have files on everyone in Atlanta?" Blade repeated in wonder.

"Comprehensive files," Eleanor replied. "A complete rundown on everyone is at our fingertips."

"Doesn't it bother you knowing that your government is maintaining a record of everything you do?" Blade inquired.

"Not at all," Eleanor answered. "We are all working toward a prosperous world," she said, sounding as if the line was memorized. "Civil rights for all means privacy for none. Privacy is selfishness."

"Can you jump through a hoop too?" Glisson cracked.

Eleanor looked at him quizzically. "A hoop?"

"Pay no attention to him," Blade said, shouldering the tramp aside. "I really would like to find my cousin as soon as possible."

"What's your cousin's name?"

"Llewellyn Snow," Blade disclosed.

"Do you know her identification number?" Eleanor queried.

"No."

"Her profession?"

"I know nothing about her except she lives in Atlanta," Blade said. "At least, that's what I was told. I hope I'm not wasting your time."

"Not at all," Eleanor assured him. "I'll ask the computer for a list of all women by that name."

"Your computer can talk?" Blade declared in alarm, thinking of the time the Warriors had encountered a hostile society in Houstin administered by a sentient "super-computer."

Eleanor chuckled. "Computers can't talk, silly. I ask our computer for imformation by typing the proper codes."

"A talking computer?" Glisson interjected, and cackled.

"This won't take but a minute," Eleanor said, walking to a nearby desk topped by a computer terminal.

"What are we going to do once we find this Snow woman?" Glisson questioned.

"We'll cross that bridge when we come to it," Blade responded.

"I can see you have this all planned out," Glisson said sarcastically.

"I'm getting tired of your complaining," Blade stated sternly. "If you figure you can do better on your own, be my guest."

"Don't be so damn touchy," Glisson remarked. "Chill out."

"It's not chilly out."

"You're hopeless. Do you know that?"

Eleanor was tapping the computer keys and staring at a green display monitor.

"Don't take this the wrong way," Glisson mentioned, "but I hope Snow isn't in the Central Directory."

Blade glanced at the tramp.

"If she isn't," Glisson added quickly, "we can get the hell out of Atlanta. And the sooner we split this burg, the healthier I'll stay."

Blade watched the Escort typing. She appeared to be puzzled, and as her fingers flew over the keys she became even more perplexed. Several minutes elapsed, until with a sigh of frustration she stood and returned to the counter. "I'm sorry," she declared.

"Why?" Blade responded.

"I'm having trouble with the computer."

"What kind of trouble?" Blade probed.

Eleanor gazed at the terminal, clearly mystified. "The Central Directory does list a Llewellyn Snow as being a resident of Atlanta—"

"Damn," Glisson grumbled.

"But I can't access the information in her life," Eleanor detailed. "I fed in the proper codes again and again, and each time the computer denied my request."

"Is that normal?" Blade asked.

"No," Eleanor answered. "We rarely have a glitch, and I've never seen anything like this. It's strange."

"So I'm stuck?"

Eleanor reflected for a moment. "Maybe not. We can always use the old-fashioned approach and let our fingers do the walking."

Blade gazed at his hands, baffled. "How do you mean?"

She reached under the counter and withdrew a thick book. "We look in the phone book. If she doesn't have an unlisted number, we could be in luck."

Glisson heard the office door open and looked back.

"Let me see," Eleanor said, flipping the pages. "H. M. R. S. Here we go." She turned the pages slowly. "I hope she's listed."

"You and me both," Blade concurred.

Glisson tapped the giant on the right shoulder.

"Not now," Blade stated, concentrating on the Escort.

Eleanor stopped on one of the pages and bent forward. "There are eight or nine Snows listed." She paused. "And here she is. Llewellyn Snow."

The old-timer was trying to drill his fingers into the Warrior's shoulder.

"Not now," Blade said testily. "What's the address?"

"Forget the address," Glisson said. "This is more important."

Blade turned, annoyed. "What could be so important?" he snapped, and then he saw the Storm Police. One stood in the doorway, and five or six more were visible in the corridor.

"Hello," said the man in the doorway. "I'm Captain Weis."

Blade straightened warily.

"Is something wrong, Captain?" Eleanor asked.

Everyone in the Visitors Bureau was staring at the officer.

"Someone in this office has been attempting to access information on Llewellyn Snow," Captain Weis declared.

"I was," Eleanor informed him.

"Why?" the officer demanded bluntly.

Eleanor indicated Blade with a nod of her head. "This man wants to contact her. She is a relative of his."

"Is that so?" Captain Weis said with a smile. He gazed at the giant. "What relation is she?"

"My cousin," Blade replied.

"Care to try again?" Captain Weis queried.

"I don't follow you," Blade declared, his right hand tucked against his pants leg, the blackjack ready for use.

"Yes, you do," Captain Weis corrected the giant. "Llewellyn Snow doesn't have a cousin. She had a brother, Richard, and a sister-in-law, Leslie, but they're both dead. And her parents were consigned to the Sleep Chambers five months ago." He paused. "So you see, the jig is up."

"Your files could be mistaken," Blade said.

"Our files are never in error," Captain Weis claimed.

Blade knew he was trapped, but he wasn't about to surrender without a struggle. He opted to stall, hoping an opening would present itself. "Then I guess there's no need for this pretense any longer." He smiled. "I'm impressed. How did you know the lady was trying to access the information?"

"Llewellyn Snow is under surveillance," Captain Weis explained. "We have put a lock on her file. If someone tries to gain entry, an alarm sounds at Storm Police headquarters. A second after this Escort tried to obtain the data, we were tracing the request. HQ immediately alerted all patrols in the area, and since we were already in the vicinity searching for a big guy with a lot of muscles and a bum, we responded. And who should we find!"

"We're dead meat," Glisson mentioned morosely.

"So we've killed two birds with one stone," Captain Weis declared contentedly. "Now we will conduct you to our headquarters."

"Where is your headquarters?" Blade inquired.

"On the third floor of the Community Directorate," Captain Weis revealed. He stepped to one side and pointed at the door. "After you."

Blade frowned as he took a stride toward the doorway.
He'd gone from the frying pan into the fire in short order.
The likelihood of contacting Llewellyn Snow was becoming
dimmer by the moment. In fact, if he didn't get his act
together, the likelihood of rejoining Hickok and Rikki was
even slimmer. He glanced at the Storm Police waiting outside of the office, then grinned at the officer.

"I'm glad you're taking this so well," Captain Weis
remarked. "I was told you might give us trouble."

"Whoever told you that was right," Blade said, and
whipped the blackjack into the startled officer's jaw.

Captain Weis went stumbling backwards and toppled
over.

One of the women in the Visitors Bureau screamed.

And Blade was in motion, bounding through the doorway
into the troopers. To his consternation, he found there were
over a half dozen in the hallway. In fact, there were more
like 20, and they swarmed upon him with the intent of
overpowering him by sheer force of numbers. The Warrior
flailed away with all of his prodigious might, striking down
trooper after trooper, feeling their blackjacks pound on his
arms, chest, neck, and shoulders. He successfully warded
off their blows to his face, with his extraordinary height
working to hinder them and limit the effectiveness of their
head strikes.

"Stay behind me!" the Warrior bellowed for Glisson's
benefit, hoping the tramp was with him.

"Get him!" one of the Storm Police was shouting, his
voice rising and bordering on hysteria. "*Get him*!"

Blade slugged a trooper on the nose, then spun and
delivered a rock-hard punch to the chin of yet another.
Between the blackjack and his left fist he was making good
headway, but the tide of battle would definitely shift in his
favor if he could reach his Bowies.

The Storm Police, however, were doggedly determined
to bring the giant down. One hit him low, around the ankles,
in an effort to tackle the Warrior.

Blade tottered, unable to take another step, and shook

his legs in an attempt to dislodge the trooper.

Seeing their adversary temporarily impeded, the rest of the Storm Police piled on him.

Blade was gripped by the wrists on both arms, but he managed to free his right arm by slamming the two troopers holding him into the wall. The respite was fleeting, as three aditional policemen took their place and clamped onto his arm for dear life. With both arms and legs rendered ineffectual, he could do nothing but utter a cry of defiance as he was buried under a milling mass of blue uniforms. "*No!*" he thundered, exerting his Herculean strength until the veins on his temples bulged. Four troopers were sent flying, but then two others struck him on the forehead with their blackjacks and the world dissolved into a galaxy of spiraling stars.

Chapter Fourteen

Hickok snapped off a hasty shot as the mutant plummeted from the rim, and before he could fire again the creature was on him. The gunman dodged to the left, evading the falling beast, although the deviate did manage to lash out with its right arm and connect with a glancing blow to the Warrior's jaw.

Chastity was shrieking in sheer terror.

The gunfighter whirled as the mutant landed upright, swiveling the M-16 barrel at the brute's midsection.

Hissing like a viper, the mutant grabbed the barrel and tore the weapon from the gunman's hands.

"Hickok!" Chastity shouted, her hands pressed to her cheeks, her eyes panic-stricken saucers.

The ape flung the M-16 to the dirt and bared its fangs.

Hickok took several swift strides backwards, his hands hovering near his Pythons, a sneer on his lips. He wanted to lure the beast farther from the girl.

Drooling and grunting, the monstrosity took the bait and lumbered after the human in buckskins.

"Hickok!" Chastity yelled once more.

"Piece of cake," the gunfighter assured her calmly. His hands flashed to the Colts, and he planted the first two shots in the creature's beady eyes, the slugs tearing into the pupils and bursting out the rear of the mutant's cranium. In a fit of pique, he shot the thing twice more in the face, each blast causing the creature to stagger and weave, and with the final round the ape toppled onto its back.

Chastity saw the gunman twirl the pearl-handled Colts into their holsters. "You did it!" she exclaimed in relief.

"There was never any doubt," Hickok said.

She ran to him and wrapped her arms around his legs. "You saved me."

Hickok leaned over and picked her up. "I'd never let anything happen to you, princess."

Chastity impulsively kissed him on the right cheek. "I love you," she blurted out.

The Warrior pecked her on the forehead. "And I reckon I'm right fond of you."

"I'd be the happiest girl in the world if you'd be my daddy," Chastity said hopefully.

"I told you that I need to ponder the notion," Hickok reminded her.

"You'll say yes," Chastity predicted.

"You sound very confident," the gunfighter observed.

"I'll pray to God," Chastity said. "Mommy always said God will answer our prayers."

Hickok looked at the rim of the pit. "Time for us to mosey on. Let's climb to the top. Hang onto my neck," he advised, squatting so she could climb aboard.

Chastity attached herself to his neck. "All set."

The Warrior reclaimed the M-16 and slung the automatic rifle over his left arm. "Here we go," he said, and gripped the pole. With deceptive ease, moving hand over hand, he ascended the shaft to the surface. After swinging his legs onto the edge, he clambered to a standing position.

"Carry me piggyback," Chastity prompted.

"I can't," Hickok said. "Climb down."

"Why can't you?" she inquired.

"I need to have my arms and hands totally free in case we're attacked again," Hickok answered. "So climb down."

"You're no fun," Chastity groused, but she slipped to the ground.

Hickok gazed at the deceased mutant. "We were fortunate. The Spirit smiled on us."

Chastity scanned the forest. "Which way do we go?"

"We head east for a spell," Hickok replied. "First we'll locate Rikki, and then we'll go after Blade."

"Which way is east?"

Hickok pointed in the appropriate direction. "The sun always rises in the east and sets in the west. Remember that, and you'll be able to keep track of your location."

Chastity went to take a step, then paused and stared at the corpse. "Where do you suppose it came from?"

"Your guess is as good as mine. Get going."

"I've never seen one like it before," Chastity remarked.

"Me neither. Let's go," Hickok urged her.

"Do you think there are more just like it?"

"Most likely," Hickok said impatiently. "Where there's one, there are bound to be others."

Chastity glanced at the vegetation. "Would they be near here?"

"Don't fret," Hickok responded. "Any other critters are miles from this spot."

A roar of unbridled rage proved the gunman wrong a moment later as a trio of mutated apes charged from the forest, converging in a feral fury on the man and the girl.

There was no time to unsling the M-16. Hickok drew the Colts and fired the right Magnum, then the left, and each shot was on target. One of the mutants was hit between the eyes and flipped backwards. The second mutant angled to the right as the Warrior fired, bearing down on Chastity, and the movement saved its life. The bullet intended for its forehead instead perforated the fleshy portion of its cheek and exited through its ear. Stunned, the beast doubled over in agony.

Chastity bolted for the woods.

Hickok pivoted and triggered the Pythons, both slugs

tearing into the third ape, ripping into its chest and spinning it around in its tracks. He thumbed the hammer on his left Colt and sent a shot into the creature's brain, and as the mutant crumpled he turned his attention to the injured ape. Too late.

The wounded brute rammed into the Warrior and encircled him with its skinny arms, the impact of its assault propelling both of them rearward.

Hickok felt his feet leave the ground, and with a start he realized they were going over the edge of the pit. The beast's lurid features were within inches of his own, its yellowish fangs spearing for his throat. If those glistening teeth didn't get him, the ten-foot plunge just might. He smashed his forehead into the ape's nostrils and twisted, jerking his body in a spin to the left, his momentum upending the creature and reversing their placement so that the mutant was on the bottom when they landed with a bone-jarring impact.

The beast released its prey, arched its back in torment, and tossed the human aside.

Hickok rolled to a stop on his abdomen, dazed, the Pythons clenched in his hands. If he didn't recover before the mutant, he was a goner. His chest ached terribly, but he suppressed the pain and forced his arms and legs to function, rising slowly and facing his bestial foe.

The mutant was already up.

Hickok elevated the Colts, his reaction sluggish, and he was unable to shoot before the ape took two steps and swung its left arm, connecting with his right temple and knocking him over.

The thing uttered a triumphant howl.

On his left side in the dirt and debris, dust swirling about him, Hickok looked up at the creature as it advanced. He raised his right arm.

With a savage snarl, the ape pounced, its knobby knees driving into the Warrior's midriff, its right fist pounding the gunman on the jaw.

Hickok nearly blacked out. A wave of vertigo washed over him, and he could taste his blood on the tip of his tongue. Another blow snapped his teeth together, and he abruptly perceived that he was on the verge of losing his life. What a stupid way to die, he mentally noted, killed by a deformed monkey!

The ape locked its fingers on the gunman's throat.

"Leave him alone, you bad monster!"

The pressure on his neck unexpectedly loosened, and Hickok took deep breaths to clear his head. He gazed upward, astonished to behold Chastity at the pit rim.

"You leave my new daddy alone!" she shouted defiantly.

Distracted by the yells, the ape was glaring at the child, its lips twitching, crimson flowing over its chin and ear.

"Leave him alone, you meany!" Chastity hollered.

The mutant roared and beat its fists on its chest.

Momentarily ignored, Hickok used the reprieve to gather his strength, feeling his senses returning to normal. He blinked rapidly, and happened to glance at the earthen floor in front of him. A tingle of excitement galvanized him as he spied a veritable godsend: the Uzi! He'd forgotten all about it during the fight!

Having decided the girl was not a threat, the ape was turning toward its original adversary.

Hickok dropped the Colts, seized the Uzi, and tucked the stock against his chest as the mutant completed its turn; he flicked off the safety as the creature bent forward; he squeezed the trigger when the ape's nails were within a hand's-breadth of his throat.

The burst stitched into the mutant and flung it backwards to crash into the pit wall, snarling insanely.

His lips compressed tightly, Hickok rose to his right knee, firing all the while, the 9-mm slugs perforating the beast's face and torso and causing it to dance like a puppet on strings. The gunfighter kept the trigger depressed until all 25 rounds in the magazine were expended, and he only ceased firing after the gun clicked empty.

The sudden silence was unnerving.

"Hickok? Are you okay?"

The Warrior licked his dry lips and looked up, mustering a weary grin. "I'm fine. Thanks to you."

"I couldn't let him hurt you," Chastity said. "You haven't made up your mind yet."

Hickok started to laugh, but an intense spasm in his left side checked his mirth. He wondered if one of his ribs was cracked or broken, and he vaguely recalled a searing pang when he fell into the pit, as if he had landed on a hard object. But the mutant had cushioned his descent. Or so he'd thought. He scanned the floor as he recovered his Colts and found the answer.

The M-16. The rifle was lying in the dirt at the exact spot of impact.

The gunman winced as he moved to the gun. He speculated that the stock of the M-16 had been wedged between the mutant's body and his own as they landed, and the weapon had slid from his shoulder before the creature had thrown him off.

"Are you coming up?" Chastity asked. "There may be more of those icky things."

Hickok snatched up the M-16 and stepped to the pole. She could be right, and he didn't want to tangle with another one of those mutants if he could help it. He aligned the Uzi over his left shoulder, the M-16 over his right, and painfully climbed from the pit.

Chastity was staring at the forest as he came over the rim.

"You saved my life, princess," Hickok said, pausing on his hands and knees. He needed to reload his weapons, but a minute of rest couldn't hurt.

Or could it.

"There's something out there," Chastity said fearfully.

Hickok pushed himself erect. "Are you sure?" he asked, and then he heard the noise too. The unmistakable sound of something approaching through the undergrowth. Blast! How many mutants were there?

Chastity moved closer to him and gripped his right pants leg. "We've got to get out of here!"

Hickok agreed. He was opening his mouth to tell her to take off when the figures materialized in the trees.

Chapter Fifteen

He wasn't certain if he was awake or dreaming. Confused, he listened to unfamiliar voices while he grappled with a strange mental fog.

". . . most extraordinary. I doubt we have his equal anywhere in the city."

"He does have superb musculature, I'll grant you that."

"We should permit the science techs to examine him."

"What? And ruin a perfect specimen by having him dissected? What a waste."

"Do you have a preference, Lilith?"

"Yes, Sol. As a matter of fact, I do."

"Then let's hear it."

"Give him to me. My psychology staff will turn him. I guarantee it."

"Is that the only reason you want him?"

"What's that supposed to mean, Clinton?"

"You don't fool us. We all know about your amorous predilection for his type."

"So? You have the same predilection."

"That's enough. Stick to the issue at hand."

"Sorry, Sol."

Blade's intellectual clarity returned in a rush. He perceived he was flat on his back, his arms and legs outstretched, his ankles and wrists secured firmly to—what?

He opened his eyes and squinted in the bright glare of brilliant overhead lights.

"Our Adonis has awakened," someone announced.

"Greetings, outsider."

Blade took his bearings as his vision adjusted. He was lying on a smooth, brown-tiled floor in the center of a circular amphitheater. A green wall eight feet in height encompassed him, and rising above the wall were twelve rows of wooden seats, each tier successively elevated. Seated on the lowest level, their heads and shoulders visible over the wall, were seven people, four men and three women, each one attired in a shimmering golden gown.

"Greetings," repeated the tallest man, a leonine figure with a mane of white hair. "I am Sol Diekrick."

Blade surveyed the seven. "You must be the Peers," he deduced.

"We are," Sol confirmed imperiously.

"He has an intellect to complement his physique," commented a woman with tresses of a sepia hue.

"Behave yourself, Lilith," remarked a portly man to her left.

"Up yours, Clinton," Lilith responded sweetly.

Sol Diekrick raised his right hand and commanded instant silence. He smiled at the giant. "My apology for the conduct of my associates. They sometimes forget themselves."

A bespectacled, gaunt man seated between Diekrick and Lilith leaned forward and glared at the prisoner. "What is your name? Where are you from?"

"My name is Jack Snow," Blade said.

"You lie!" snapped the man with the glasses. "We know you gave that fabrication to the Storm Police, but our files indicate there never was a cousin of Llewellyn Snow by the name of Jack."

"Your computer is incorrect."

"Our computer system is virtually infallible, you primitive!"

"Eldred, please control yourself," Sol interjected in a paternal tone. He smiled down at the Warrior. "You must forgive our lack of manners."

Blade glanced at his wrists and found wide strips of an orange material binding him to the floor.

Sol noticed. "Simply a security precaution, I assure you, necessitated by your disinclination to cooperate with duly constituted authorities."

"In other words," Lilith said with a smirk, "we had to tie you up because the Storm Police were afraid you'd strangle us to death."

Blade thought of the tramp. "Where's Glisson?"

"Who?" Sol replied. "Oh. You mean the filthy degenerate taken into custody with you? He's being held in a cell until we have rendered a final disposition of your case."

"Where am I?" Blade asked.

"You are in the Civil Directorate," Sol Diekrick answered. "My Directorate. You're on the ninth floor in a room we reserve for special interrogations."

"How long was I out?"

"A few hours," Sol divulged. "Your recuperative powers are amazing. You must have exceptional stamina."

"I'll bet that's not all he has," Lilith said.

Sol sighed and leaned back. "Allow me to introduce my associates. Lilith Friekan here, the one with the raging hormones, heads the Orientation Directorate."

Lilith grinned and winked.

"Eldred Morley is in charge of the Euthanasia Directorate," Sol revealed.

The man with the glasses scowled at the Warrior.

Dietrich nodded at the portly Peer. "Clinton Brigg handles Ethics."

"Hi, handsome," Brigg remarked.

"As for the rest," Sol said, and indicated a brunette, "Rebecca Sanger heads the Life Directorate." He pointed at a man with black hair and a cleft chin. "Alec Toine has

Progress."

Toine nodded.

"And last, but definitely not least," Sol said, gazing at an elderly woman with aquiline features, "Dorothy Coinnak is responsible for the Community Directorate."

Blade studied each of them critically, then shook his head.

"What is it?" Sol inquired.

The Warrior stared at Diekrick. "Appearances can be deceiving. All of you appear to be sane."

"Implying we are not," Sol said.

"You're warped."

Sol chuckled and rested his chin in his right hand on the wall. "By whose standards? Yours?"

"By anyone's standards," Blade replied. "I've seen and heard enough to convince me that you're either off the deep end, or all of you are power-hungry, petty dictators."

"We are neither," Sol stated.

"Says you."

Eldred Morley stood. "Let's dispose of this cretin now, Sol. Why should we sit here and allow him to insult us?"

"Sit down, Eldred," Sol Diekrick ordered.

Morley reluctantly complied.

"That's better," Sol said. "Your immaturity is appalling. If you can't rebut the arguments of a musclebound oaf, perhaps you don't deserve to hold the exalted post of Peer."

Morley blanched. "I didn't mean—"

"I know what you meant," Sol said, cutting him short. "And don't insult *my* intelligence ever again."

"I won't," Morley said hastily.

Sol looked at the giant. "Now where were we? Ahhh, yes. You claim that we're warped, as you so quaintly phrased it."

"Convince me otherwise," Blade stated.

Diekrick folded his arms across his chest. "You erred when you accused us of being petty dictators. We actually view the welfare of our people as our paramount concern."

Blade laughed.

"You don't believe me?"

"You have the people of Atlanta right where you want them," Blade mentioned. "Under your thumb. This Civil Council has stripped the citizens of their freedom. You control every aspect of their lives. You decide what is best for them, and you've even gone so far as to regulate the clothes they wear." He paused. "You're disgusting."

"My dear fellow, you misconstrue our intent," Sol said with an air of condescension. "And your knowledge of America is deficient."

"America?"

"Yes. Specifically the history of America in the decades preceding World War Three. We have merely continued and improved upon the reforms instituted by our ancestors, and we have succeeded in achieving the goal they dreamed of."

"What goal?" Blade queried.

"The creation of the world's first fully humanistic society," Sol said loftily. "America was becoming increasingly humanistic with each generation. The humanists were effectively organized, and the rank and file, the masses on the street, had no idea what was happening to them. The average American didn't know that most of their leaders, their politicians and educators, were humanists. They were unaware that humanism was the prevalent doctrine at a majority of the universities and colleges. Had they known, they would have rebelled because they were strongly opposed to everything humanism stands for."

"And what does humanism stand for?" Blade questioned.

"Read the humanist manifestos," Sol replied. "The humanists made no secret of their beliefs, only of the means they employed to restructure society. Humanism has certain basic tenets. There is no God, no spirit reality of any kind. Prayer and worship are meaningless practices, and consequently we have outlawed them. Humanism asserts religion is an obstacle to human progress, not an aid." He paused and gazed thoughtfully at the Warrior. "The early humanists clearly outlined the design for a secular society, and we've implemented their design. Religion has been eliminated. Science is our guidepost and experience our teacher. Our moral values and ethics are not limited by childish concepts of right and wrong. There is no right and wrong. There is only the good life, what we feel is best for us at any given moment. The quest for the good life is good for all.''

"And you really believe all that garbage?''

"Wholeheartedly,'' Sol responded. "Our society is perfect. Our citizens can satisfy their every need and interest. If it doesn't harm others, they're free to do whatever they want consistent with their civil liberties. Sexual expression, abortion, birth control, divorce, you name it.''

"So long as the people obey your laws, there's no problem,'' Blade said.

"Every civilized society has laws,'' Sol noted.

"But not every civilized society uses laws to enslave its people.''

"I can see this is getting us nowhere,'' Sol declared. He glanced at the other Peers. "We should proceed to the formal disposition of the subject.''

"At last,'' Morely commented.

"Give him to Orientation,'' Lilith proposed. "We'll probe his mind, uncover his innermost secrets.''

"I say immediate termination is best,'' Morley suggested.

"We should learn more about him first,'' Alec Toine said. "Where does he come from? Why did he want to see Llewellyn Snow? What connection does he have to Richard Snow?''

"I agree,'' Sol declared. "This man is a mystery, and I don't like mysteries.'' He smiled at the giant. "I don't suppose you'd be willing to answer all of our questions.''

"I don't suppose you'd be willing to jump off this building,'' Blade responded.

Sol reached down and produced the Bowies. "The Storm Police found these when they were binding you. You must have a fetish for large knives.''

"The better to gut you with, Grandma," Blade quipped.

Diekrick hefted the twin knives. "You won't cooperate with us. We could use drugs to elicit the information I want, but someone with your willpower and constitution could resist indefinitely. I don't intend to wait."

"What will we do?" Lilith asked.

"There is a better way," Sol said, smirking at the Warrior. "You *will* tell me everything I want to know."

"What makes you think so?" Blade countered.

Sol Diekrick leaned over the lip of the wall, grinning wickedly. "Let me put it to you this way. How do you feel about weenie roasts?"

Chapter Sixteen

"Are you sure those two will take good care of the princess?"

"Scarlet and Jane will protect Chastity with their lives."

"Have they ever baby-sat before?"

Locklin looked at the gunfighter in annoyance. "Will you give me a break? Chastity is in good hands." He hurried ahead, muttering. "You'd think you were her father, the way you act!"

"Now what in the blazes got into that yahoo?" Hickok asked.

Rikki-Tikki-Tavi, walking on the gunman's right, grinned. "You like the child, don't you?"

"I reckon I'm a mite fond of her," Hickok confessed. "She saved my hide yesterday."

"So you've said," Rikki mentioned. "About three dozen times."

"I was tickled pink when I saw you walk into the clearing," Hickok said. "Another ape would've driven me bananas."

Rikki glanced at his friend. "Have you made your decision yet?"

"She told you?"

"Last night, when we were sitting around the campfire," Rikki disclosed. "She calls me Uncle Rikki now."

"Well, Uncle Rikki, I need your advice."

"*You* are asking for advice?" Rikki responded in surprise.

"What's the big deal?"

"You never ask for advice," Rikki said.

"I'm askin' now."

"The decision is yours," Rikki stated.

Hickok frowned. "Remind me to never ask for your advice again."

"I wouldn't want to be in your shoes," Rikki added.

"Are you tryin' to cheer me up or depress me?" the gunman asked.

"I just want to help."

Hickok made a snorting sound. "If you call this helpin', I'd hate to see it when you're being wishy-washy."

"Will you two clowns keep the noise down?" Locklin snapped over his right shoulder.

"Cranky cuss, isn't he?" Hickok said. He scanned the forest ahead, noting the point men 30 yards away, then stared along their back trail at the 32 men and women in green trudging toward the metropolis. Periodic breaks in the foliage enabled him to see the skyscrapers several miles distant.

"We should be there before nightfall," Locklin announced.

Hickok gazed at the afternoon sun. "We should have gone in this morning."

Locklin heard the comment and slowed to hike alongside the Warriors. "Trying to enter the city in broad daylight would be suicide."

"I hope this plan of yours works," Hickok said.

The rebel leader's eyes narrowed. "Don't you like me?"

"Why would you say that?" Hickok responded.

"You've been so critical of every decision I've made," Locklin mentioned. "You didn't like the idea of leaving Chastity with Scarlet and Jane, and you griped about my plan to wait until an hour before the Civil Council meeting to enter Atlanta."

"It's nothin' personal," Hickok assured him. "I'm worried about my pard, is all."

"If your friend, Blade, is still alive, we'll find him," Locklin promised.

"If Blade isn't alive, the Peers will regret the day they were born," Hickok said.

They reached a field.

Locklin double-checked to insure the sky was clear of planes before giving the signal to advance.

"I've been meanin' to ask you something," Hickok said as they started to cross.

"What is it?" Locklin responded.

"We have this gigantic library at our Home. When I was knee high to a whippoorwill, I spent many an hour readin' all kinds of books. Westerns were my favorite, but I read other kinds. And one of them was about this gent who lived centuries ago in England. He was famous for robbin' from the rich and givin' to the poor. Like you, he was partial to the bow and arrow. Like you, he wore green all the time. And like you, he had a band of—what were they called?— happy hunters who would follow him anywhere." Hickok hooked his thumbs in his gunbelt. "Any connection?"

Locklin had listened with a smile spreading over his countenance. "You surprise me. Very few people know about Robin Hood."

"Then there is a connection?"

"I came across a book on him and decided to emulate his style," Locklin detailed. "Robin Hood was a master of the hit-and-run, a true guerrilla fighter. I patterned my band after him, and I gave each of them a code name based on the book. The Peers don't know who some of us are, and there's no reason to make their identification of us an easy job. Many of us have relatives living in the city, and to protect them we screen our true identities."

"What's your real name?" Hickok asked.

"Matthew. Matthew Brody."

Hickok looked over his left shoulder at the one they called Big John. "And him?"

"His real name is Harold Cridlebaugh."

"I should've known," the gunman said.

"Speaking of questions," Rikki interjected, "there is an issue we haven't discussed yet."

"What is it?" Locklin responded.

"What will happen if you slay the Peers?"

"The people of Atlanta will finally be free," Locklin said. "There will be celebrating in the streets."

"Will there?"

"I don't follow you," Locklin stated.

"Is your small band representative of the populace of Atlanta?" Rikki probed. "Do you speak for a majority of the people, or are you in the minority? If you kill the Peers, what next? Will the people rise up to support you? Will new Peers arise? How will the Storm Police react? Will they stand idly by, or will they be actively involved in the redistribution of power?" He paused. "What will happen?"

Locklin pursed his lips and gazed absently at the ground. "I honestly don't know," he commented at length. "There are many people who resent the Peers and want a new government, but there are also many citizens satisfied with the status quo. I don't know what will happen."

"Those Storm galoots could pose a problem for you," Hickok remarked. "How will you deal with them? Killin' the Peers won't solve a thing if the Storm Police don't side with you."

"I've heard a rumor that the chief of the Storm Police, a man named Skinner, resents the Peers and wants them disposed of," Locklin said.

"Rumors do not a revolution make," Rikki philosophized.

"We can't worry about the Storm Police now," Locklin declared. "First things first. First, the Peers. We'll tend to the Storm Police when the time comes."

"I hope you know what you're doing," Hickok said.

They finished traversing the field in contemplative silence, then hiked into another stretch of forest.

"I'd like to hear the plan again," Hickok mentioned.

"We've already gone over our strategy twice," Locklin responded.

"Humor me."

The rebel leader sighed and scratched his beard. "The Civil Council meets in the Civil Directorate once a week at nine P.M. Their meeting chamber is located on the tenth floor of the Directorate. All we have to do is wait until eight, enter the city through the storm drains, and reach the Civil Directorate without being spotted. There should be a service elevator we can take to the tenth floor. Very few guards should be on duty because the Peers won't be expecting any trouble."

"It's awful risky," Hickok remarked.

"Do you have a better idea?" Locklin retorted. "If you want to save your friend, pray this works."

They marched westward as the sun dipped toward the horizon. Splendid tints of red, orange, and pink lent a grandeur to the sunset.

"I hope Chastity is okay," Hickok commented at one point.

As the band drew ever nearer to the sprawling metropolis, they proceeded with heightened caution. Their green apparel enabled them to blend into the landscape, and they stealthily approached to within a hundred yards of the wall. Locklin gestured, and his followers instantly fanned out in a skirmish line from north to south. Putting his finger over his lips, Locklin led the two Warriors to a cluster of thick brush 70 yards from the city. He crouched and peered at the rampart.

"I count three guards," he said.

"Four," Rikki corrected him. "See the one to the right?"

Locklin looked and nodded. "You have good eyes."

"But his nose is too big," Hickok quipped.

"Where are the storm drains?" Rikki inquired.

"You can't see them from here," Locklin said. "There are two of them at the base of the wall, hidden in those tall weeds."

"What about those coyotes on the wall?" Hickok asked.

Locklin consulted a watch on his left wrist. "My archers are already in position. In five minutes they'll take the guards out."

The gunman scrutinized the western horizon. "It won't be dark for another half hour, at least."

"It's July," Locklin said. "It doesn't get dark until nine. But it will be on the dim side. Dusk usually is," he concluded wryly.

The light was gradually fading as the sun began to sink out of sight.

Hickok checked the magazine in the Uzi, and saw Rikki doing the same.

On the wall, oblivious to the presence of the rebels, the guards went about their business. Two were engaged in conversation, while the remaining pair were conducting slow patrols of the rampart, one moving to the north, one to the south. All four were armed with AR-15s.

The gunman watched the tableau unfold, and he felt a degree of admiration for the skill the rebels displayed. With unerring accuracy, four arrows were released at the same moment and sped true to the respective target. Four shafts penetrated four hearts, and four forms sprawled onto the rampart.

"Now," Locklin whispered, then held his right fist aloft. His band converged on the wall in an orderly, quiet dash.

Hickok and Rikki stayed abreast of Locklin. They waited as his men used long knives to slash an opening in the weeds, exposing a set of man-sized storm drains.

"They're barred," Rikki observed.

"No problem," Locklin stated confidently, and nodded at three of his men. Each one carried a large, brown leather pouch, and from the pouch each pulled out a hacksaw. "Get to it," he directed.

The trio applied themselves to the bars of the left-hand drain, their sawing sounding like the buzzing of a swarm of bees.

Hickok surveyed the rampart, his fingers on the Uzi trigger.

"The Storm Police assign their guards to a specific sector on the wall," Locklin explained. "The ones we killed aren't due to be relieved until midnight, and my men are keeping an eye on the guards north and south of here."

"These bars are tough," one of the men sawing commented.

"Don't stop," Locklin said. "We're on a tight schedule."

Hickok gazed into the gloomy drain. "Where does this oversized gopher hole lead?"

"These were installed after the war, when the climate changed," Locklin answered. "Atlanta began receiving twice as much annual rainfall. The experts claimed a shift in the jet stream was to blame. Anyway, right now we're between Rock Springs Road and La Vista. The drains lead to the Atlanta Water Works Reservoirs, to channel the overflow during the rainy season. One of the branches will lead us to within a block of the Civil Directorate. We won't have to worry about the Storm Police."

"Good," Hickok said.

"We'll just need to watch out for the rats, the spiders, and the tunnel mutants."

"The what?" Hickok asked.

"Thousands of rats and spiders live in the drains," Locklin detailed. "A lot are drowned during the runoff, but somehow they always multiply like rabbits afterwards."

"And the tunnel mutants?"

"Mutants are everywhere. You know that. The storm drains are no exception," Locklin said.

"You have used the drains before," Rikki deduced.

"Yes," Locklin confirmed. "We used them regularly to sneak into the city until about a year ago. Then the Storm Police caught on and installed bars on every drain."

"Has anyone ever seen mutant apes in the drains?" Hickok inquired.

"Not to my knowledge," Locklin replied. "Why?"

"Oh, nothin'."

The three men were sawing at a frantic pace.

Locklin checked his watch again. "We're falling behind schedule." He nodded at three of his band. "Take over for them."

A woman in green raced up to them. "More guards are coming!" she declared.

"Where?" Locklin asked.

"From the north," the woman disclosed. "Two of them."

"How far off?"

"Five hundred yards or better."

"Have everyone take cover," Locklin commanded. "Take three with you. I want these guards stopped before they get too close. Use two archers for each guard."

"I understand," the woman acknowledged. She pointed at three rebels, and together they sprinted northward. The rest crouched low.

"Keep sawing," Locklin told the men at the drain. "The guards are too far off to hear us."

"Do you think they know we're here?" Big John inquired.

"They have no way of knowing," Locklin said.

Hickok stared to the north, pleased to notice the increasingly murky light.

Working strenuously, the men at the drain grunted and huffed.

The gunman gazed at the Freedom Fighters, regarding their determined, courageous expressions. Face after face conveyed a grim sense of purpose.

All except for one.

Hickok studied the singular exception, a young man with blue eyes and blond hair. What was his name again? Rikki had introduced them the night before. Dale. That was it. The youth was gnawing nervously on his lower lip and gazing apprehensively at the woods to their rear.

Why?

The gunman focused on the vegetation, searching in the shadows for signs of life.

Nothing.

Footsteps pounded on the turf and the woman returned. "More Storm Police!" she declared, out of breath.

"How many?" Locklin demanded.

"I lost count," she responded. "I left the others to keep watch. There are dozens of police coming from the north."

Another runner suddenly arrived from the south. "Locklin! Storm Police!"

"How many?"

"Over three dozen," the second runner disclosed.

"What the hell is going on?" Locklin commented. "They can't know we're here."

Hickok saw the youth swallow hard. "I wouldn't bank on that, bucko."

"Why?" Locklin asked in consternation.

Before Hickok could reply, the men at the drain removed a quarter of the barred grate.

"Locklin!" someone shouted. "The trees!"

As one, all the Freedom Fighters turned to discover the forest abruptly infested with a horde of Storm Police.

"*Rebel scum*!" a gruff voice bellowed, the speaker using a megaphone. "*Drop your weapons and surrender, or you will die where you stand*!"

Chapter Seventeen

"I trust that you enjoyed your rest?" Sol Diekrick said.

"I didn't expect such plush accommodations," Blade admitted, thinking of the holding cell in which he'd spent the day, a cell furnished with a comfortable bed, a table and chair, and even a portable radio. Three meals had been served, all piping hot. He had stubbornly resisted eating the first two, but his gnawing hunger had persuaded him to eat a portion of the evening repast. The cell, to the best of his estimation, was located in an underground level of the Civil Directorate. Less than five minutes ago 20 Storm Police had arrived to escort him to the Peers.

"We're not barbarians, after all," Sol declared archly.

Blade took stock of his surroundings. He was ten feet from a long metal table, the door to the room at his back. Seated and eyeing him intently were all the Peers, with Sol Diekrich at the head of the table to the right. Beyond the table was an unusual glass pane, allowing those in the room to gaze over a huge chamber below. Peculiar roofless walls filled the enormous expanse.

"I was told you ate sparingly," Sol mentioned. "Wasn't our cuisine adequate?" The Bowies were on the table in front of him.

"I'm on a diet," Blade quipped.

"You look fine to me," Lilith Friekan remarked from her chair at the left end of the table.

"Behave, my dear," Sol advised.

"Why have you spared me?" Blade asked.

"You're complaining?" Sol rejoined.

"I was under the impression you wanted information, and fast," Blade said.

"I did, initially," Sol confessed. "But before we could arrange our special entertainment, we received news affecting you directly. I decided to delay the entertainment until the appropriate time."

"I don't understand," Blade stated.

"You will," Sol declared with a smirk. He glanced at the Storm Police captain in charge of the 20-man detail. "Have your men file into this room along the walls. I want our guest to refrain from interfering with our entertainment, and your presence should deter him."

The captain nodded and obeyed.

"Now where was I?" Sol commented.

"What news?" Blade inquired, flexing his wrist muscles to test the handcuffs restraining his arms.

"In due time," Sol said. "First, our entertainment for the evening. You are receiving quite an honor. We have disrupted our normal schedule for this event."

"Lucky me," Blade cracked.

Sol swiveled in his chair and nodded at the chamber below. "Any idea what that is?"

"You're adding to the building and haven't finished this level yet?" Blade guessed.

"Wrong," Sol said.

Blade shrugged. "From up here, it looks like a giant rat maze," he speculated, partially in jest.

"How astute of you," Sol complimented him. "Yes, it is a maze."

Blade's levity vanished. He stared at the network of walls, his forehead furrowing, disturbed by the implications.

"If you'll notice," Sol went on, "we are able to view the entire maze from up here. We have ringside seats, so to speak."

"For what?"

"Take a close look at those walls," Sol suggested. "Tell me what you see."

Blade moved over to the table and peered at the maze. He'd assumed the walls were wooden; now he realized the outer surface of each wall was covered with a dull brown material unlike any other he knew. "What is that?"

"A fireproof fabric we use to protect the inner metal walls," Sol divulged.

"Fireproof?"

"Yes," Sol said, leaning back in his chair and smiling smugly. "Perhaps I should explain. Do you see the two doors?"

Blade surveyed the chamber, discovering a door in the middle of the wall on the far right and another door in a corresponding position on the left. "Yeah."

"Those doors allow our players to enter the maze," Sol detailed.

"This is some sort of game?" Blade asked.

"Yes. A game of life and death," Sol said.

Blade glanced at Diekrick.

"We've decided to put on a demonstration in your honor," Sol stated.

"Don't put yourselves out on my account," Blade commented.

"It's no bother, I assure you," Sol said.

"Let's begin the show," Clinton Brigg suggested.

"What's the rush?" Sol responded. "We have all night. And we want to be here when our other guests arrive."

"I wish we had some popcorn," Eldred Morley remarked.

Sol looked at the giant. "Let's introduce the players for tonight." He rose and walked to the gigantic glass pane, stopping next to a control panel on the right-hand wall at the junction with the pane.

"I hope the Terminators don't end it too quickly," Lilith mentioned.

"Come here," Sol said, beckoning the Warrior.

Blade moved around the table to the glass pane, to the

left of Diekrick. He gazed at the maze, dreading the worst.

"An old friend of yours is one of the participants," Sol said. His right hand reached out and he pressed a red button on the control panel.

Blade saw one of the doors in the maze, the one on the far right, open by sliding into a recessed slot. And there, shuffling into the maze, being prodded by two Storm Police with blackjacks, was the hobo, Glisson.

"It's your buddy," Sol stated sarcastically.

"What do you plan to do to him?" Blade queried.

"*We* won't do a thing," Sol replied. "You will."

"Me?"

"Yes. I'll elucidate after I present the opposing players." Sol depressed an orange button on the panel, and the door on the left side of the maze promptly opened.

Blade's abdominal muscles tensed.

Four figures attired in shining silver outfits strolled into sight. The head and neck of each was covered by unique headgear with dark, tinted eyepieces. Strapped to the back of each was a trio of thin tanks, and clutched in the hands of each was a flared, gunlike nozzle.

"A Terminator squad," Sol said. "Perhaps you're familiar with the reputation our Terminators have? A richly deserved reputation, I might add. Their Fryers are extremely lethal."

Blade did not respond. He glanced from the Terminators, waiting patiently near the left-hand door, to Glisson, who was wringing his hands nervously in front of the right-hand entrance.

"You can't see it from here, but there is a yellow light affixed to the wall above this glass pane," Sol advised. "If I press this brown button"—and he indicated the appropriate button on the control panel—"the yellow light will come on and the festivities will commence."

Blade still said nothing.

"The rules are very simple," Sol explained. "The Terminators enter the maze from the left, and your friend enters the maze from the right. If your friend manages to negotiate the maze and reaches the door on the left, he wins the most valuable prize imaginable: his life." Sol paused. "If, however, the Terminators find Glisson before he reaches the opposite side of the chamber, then they will fry him on the spot. Simple enough, don't you think?"

"You bastard."

"Spare me your juvenile insults," Sol stated.

"Glisson doesn't stand a chance," Blade remarked bitterly.

"On the contrary, he does," Sol said. "Believe it or not, some players have reached the other side safely. The Terminators do not possess an unfair advantage. They do not have the maze memorized, if that's what you're thinking."

"The odds are four to one," Blade protested. "And the Terminators are armed with flamethrowers. You call that fair?"

Sol shrugged. "As fair as his type deserves."

Blade glared at the Peer.

"There is always the possibility Glisson will be spared," Sol said. "We could call the whole thing off."

"What does Glisson have to do?" Blade asked.

"Him? Not a thing," Sol said. "Whether he plays our little game or not is up to you."

"Me?"

"You," Sol reiterated, his tone lowering. "I want information. I want to know all about you: your name, where you are from, the reason you're in Atlanta, everything. If you supply this information, Glisson gets free."

The Warrior gazed at the aged tramp.

"You were eager to find Llewellyn Snow. I want to know why," Sol declared. "Llewellyn Snow is under constant surveillance while we debate whether to consign her to a Sleep Chamber. Her brother, Richard, published *The Atlanta Tribune* until recently. We were forced to eradicate him."

"What did he do?" Blade inquired.

"The fool intended to publish an editorial critical of us,"

Sol snapped. "We exercise creative authority over all the media in the city—"

"You censor them," Blade interrupted.

"—and all editorials must be officially sanctioned prior to publication," Sol continued, unfazed. "Snow planned to slip one into his paper without our knowledge, but fortunately one of his staff blew the whistle."

"So you had him killed over an editorial?"

"You should have seen it!" Sol said. "Snow accused us of being arbitrary and despotic. After twelve years as publisher, after receiving favored status, he turned on us."

"Why?"

Sol made a snorting sound. "Over the merest trifle. His parents were consigned to the Sleep Chambers five months ago, after they turned sixty-six. According to our law, that's the cut-off age. All those over sixty-six are rated as past their prime, burdens on society, and incapable of producing enough to justify the expense of extending their life span."

"Snow turned against you after his parents were murdered," Blade commented sarcastically. "How could he be so ungrateful?"

"His wife attempted to flee the city with their only child, a girl," Sol said. "The Terminators caught the mother, thanks to a tip from Llewellyn."

Blade was shocked. "Llewellyn Snow betrayed her sister-in-law?"

"Llewellyn knew her life was in jeopardy because of her brother's treachery. To prove her worth, she notified us of Leslie Snow's plans," Sol answered. "We sent a Terminator squad after her. The mother was fried, but the child escaped. The Terminators searched and searched, but the child eluded them." He sighed. "Hopefully, the girl perished in the wilderness. The Snow bloodline is genetically inferior and deserves to be eradicated."

"Does this include Llewellyn Snow?" Blade asked.

"She did not condone her brother's treachery," Diekrick said. "And she did inform on Leslie. If our monitoring of her activities does not uncover any latent deviation, she will be spared."

"How sweet of you," Blade quipped.

"Now to the matter at hand," Sol declared. "What will it be?"

"My freedom would be nice."

"Don't indulge your infantile humor at my expense!" Sol snapped. "You know very well what I mean. Will you provide the information I want, or does Glisson face the maze?"

Blade gazed at the labyrinth, the Terminators, and finally the hobo. He doubted Gilsson could survive the contest, and he was tempted to answer all of Sol's questions. But his primary responsibility was to the Family and the Home; if he gave Diekrick everything the Peer wanted, he would be betraying the trust of those who relied upon him. There was no telling what the Peers would do. They might decide to send a demolition or commando team to destroy the Home, which had already survived assaults by scavengers, mutants, Russians, the Doktor's forces, Trolls, and others. Under no circumstances would he endanger the compound again.

"What will it be?" Sol demanded once more.

"Go sit on a pitchfork."

"You have sealed his doom," Sol said, and pressed the brown button.

Reacting instantly, as if they were eager to commence, the four Terminators entered the maze.

Glisson was shoved by the two Storm Police. He nearly fell, glared at them, then walked into the network of confusing passageways. The Storm Police exited through the right-hand door, which promptly closed.

"At last!" Eldred Morley exclaimed.

Blade's gray eyes narrowed as he studied the maze, following the progress of the Terminators and Glisson. From his vantage point, thanks to the elevation of the room, he could see all five participants, but only from the waist up. Their lower extremities were obscured by the six-foot-high walls.

"I wager the bum doesn't last ten minutes," Clinton Brigg commented.

"I'll take you up on that," Lilith said.

"Do you feel like talking yet?" Sol asked the Warrior.

Blade shook his head, his arm muscles tensed, seemingly anxious for Glisson's safety but surreptitiously straining on the handcuffs.

"Suit yourself," Sol stated, gazing at the maze.

The Terminators had separated, taking different branches. Glisson was proceeding at a snail's pace, fearfully looking around every corner before venturing into the next passage.

"What a timid mouse," Sol said contemptuously.

"I'd like to see how brave you'd be," Blade commented.

Diekrick laughed. "Never happen."

Blade looked at the metal table to his left, at the glass pane, then at the Storm Police ringing the walls, calculating distances and odds. He estimated the nearest trooper was 15 feet away; the table was only six feet off; and the space between the end of the table and the glass pane was a mere yard.

"Hey! The scum has stopped," Morley complained.

Indeed, Glisson had halted at an intersection and was appraising each option with transparent anxiety.

"What happens if he goes back?" Blade inquired.

"Back to where he started?" Sol asked.

Blade nodded.

"The Terminators are empowered to fry him anywhere in the chamber, even by the door," Sol disclosed. "His best bet is to keep moving and not to lose his sense of direction."

"That pathetic excuse for a human couldn't find his butt in the dark with both hands," Morley cracked.

Blade glanced casually at the table again. "Why did you bring my Bowies?"

"To make the next contest more challenging," Sol replied.

"You're sending me in there next?"

Diekrick grinned maliciously. "I'm a patient man, but my patience is not unlimited. If you won't divulge the information I want, then you will be next. A fresh Terminator squad will be sent in, and it will be their flamethrowers against your Bowies." He chuckled. "We anticipate great entertainment."

"I hope I don't disappoint you," Blade remarked.

"I hope our other guests arrive in time," Sol said.

Blade stepped up to the pane, watching Glisson take a passage to the tramp's left. He assessed the span from the pane to the floor below at 20 feet. For someone of his stature, 20 feet wasn't insurmountable. The falling glass, though, would pose a definite hazard. If he could—

Wait a second.

What was this?

Blade inspected the pane minutely for several moments. "This isn't glass," he declared.

Sol Diekrick appeared amused by the observation. "Of course it isn't. Glass became outdated decades before the war because of its nasty habit of cutting people when broken. Substitutes were quite common. This substance, for instance, is called Polyperv." He tapped the pane. "It has all of the positive qualities of glass, but it doesn't contain the same flaws. When Polyperv shatters, the fragments tend to be large instead of fractured splinters as with glass. And the fragments have a duller edge than with glass. A person is less likely to be cut."

"Interesting," Blade remarked. "I remember reading about bullet-proof substances, virtually shatterproof, used prior to the Big Blast. Is this one of those substances?"

"Polyperv? No. Why would we bother to install an expensive bulletproof panel here? The pane is highly fire resistant, though," Sol responded.

"How convenient," Blade said, taking a step to his left,

a step closer to the table.

And his Bowies.

"Why this intense interest in the window?" Sol asked. "Don't you care if Glisson lives or dies?"

Blade nodded, taking another stride, his eyes on the maze. "Of course I care."

"You could have fooled me," Sol said.

"I hope to," Blade replied, and glanced at the doorway to the room. "Who's the guy with the machine gun?"

It was one of the oldest tricks in the book, and the Warrior performed the ruse flawlessly. By conveying an attitude of nonchalance, and by phrasing his question casually, he succeeded in temporarily diverting the attention of everyone in the room to the door. In the few seconds required for them to realize there was no one there, he accomplished his goal.

Blade's massive arm muscles bulged, his shoulders rippling, as he exerted all of his strength. His features reddened and his teeth clenched, and with a loud crack the links connecting the cuffs parted. Before the Peers and the Storm Police could perceive his purpose, he leaped to the table and grabbed the Bowies.

"Get him!" Sol Diekrick bellowed.

The Storm Police rushed the giant.

Chapter Eighteen

"Where did they come from?" one of the Freedom Fighters cried.

"We're trapped!" yelled another.

"Into the storm drain!" Locklin ordered, motioning at the opening in the grate.

Dozens of bright beams of light caught the Freedom Fighters in a stark glare as the Storm Police produced flashlights.

"*Drop your weapons!*" the man with the megaphone repeated. "*Now!*"

Locklin gripped Hickok's right arm and pushed the Warrior toward the drain. "Go!"

"We're not leavin' you," Hickok said.

"Some of us can escape through the drain, but we must move quickly. Now go!" Locklin snapped.

Rikki-Tikki-Tavi surveyed the scene, noting the Storm Police steadily advancing with their automatic rifles at the ready and the compact mass of rebels with their backs, literally, to the wall. He moved to the grate and crouched in front of the hole in the bars. "Come on," he said to the gunman, then slid inside.

Hickok hesitated. "My irons can come in handy."

"This is not your fight," Locklin responded, keeping his gaze on the Storm Police. "It's ours. And you have your friend to think of. Go! Please! We'll be right behind you."

"Hurry," Rikki prompted from within the drain.

Frowning in annoyance, the gunfighter entered the storm drain and moved a few feet inward to join Rikki. He found he could stand, although the height of the culvert did not permit him to straighten entirely.

Locklin poked his head inside. "Take off! We'll hold them as long as we can."

"May the Spirit preserve you," Rikki said, and headed deeper into the drain.

Hickok reluctantly followed his friend. The interior was obscured in inky blackness and the tunnel ahead was indistinguishable. "Why are we desertin' them?" he demanded.

"Blade must come first," Rikki replied.

"I know, but—" Hickok began.

"If we had stayed, we would die with them," Rikki stated.

Gunfire erupted from their rear, commingled with screams and curses.

"We can't abandon them," Hickok objected, and unexpectedly bumped into his companion in the dark. "Why'd you stop?"

"Locklin gave me this," Rikki said, and a small flame sparked to life, illuminating the drain for a yard or so in both directions.

"What is it?"

"A lighter. We must hurry," Rikki reiterated, and hastened on.

The sounds of the conflict had reached a crescendo.

"I still say we shouldn't abandon them," Hickok groused.

"Would you rather abandon Blade?"

"Of course not," Hickok replied.

"Then we have no choice," Rikki stressed. "They were hopelessly outnumbered. Our guns would not have made a difference."

"It rankles me to walk out on folks I like," Hickok remarked. "We'd better not make a habit of this."

"We won't," Rikki assured him.

The Warriors lost all track of time and distance as they penetrated farther and farther into the storm drain. The sounds of battle grew fainter, and eventually faded.

"Do you know which way to go?" Hickok asked.

"Locklin gave me directions."

"Why didn't he tell me?"

"You were busy relating a bedtime story to Chastity," Rikki said.

"If anything happens to her . . ." Hickok stated, leaving the sentence unfinished.

They continued in silence for a long time.

"Wait," Hickok directed.

Rikki stopped. "What is it?"

"I thought I heard something," Hickok mentioned, turning to view the drain to their rear.

"What?"

"I'm not sure, pard."

The pad of rushing feet filled the conduit.

"Could be the Storm Police," Hickok whispered, leveling the Uzi.

"We should keep going," Rikki advised.

"You can skedaddle if you want," Hickok declared. "But I'm not runnin' twice in one night. It'd give me a complexion."

"Don't you mean a complex?"

"Whatever."

"It could be a mutant," Rikki mentioned.

"I hope so."

"You do?"

"I'm in the mood to blow something away, and it might as well be a blasted mutant," Hickok stated. "Flick off the lighter."

Rikki complied, and they stood in total darkness and waited as the footsteps became progressively louder.

Unexpectedly, the noise ceased.

An interval of quiet engulfed the drain.

"Psst! Hickok? Rikki? Are you there?"

The gunman recognized the voice and smiled. "Yeah, we're here, Locklin."

Rikki ignited the lighter.

"There you are!" Locklin called, and a second later the dim figure of the rebel leader and others hastened toward the Warriors.

"Glad you made it," Hickok said.

"Not half as glad as I am," Locklin responded. Fourteen of his band were with him, and five of them sported gunshot wounds. One was limping.

"Where are the rest?" Rikki inquired.

Locklin slowed when he was a few yards off, his expression sad, and slowly shook his head.

"And the Storm Police?" Hickok questioned, spying Big John and the youth named Dale behind Locklin.

"They closed in on us from the forest and the rampart," the rebel leader said. "We took down twenty or so, but they were getting our range and my people were dropping right and left. I decided to live to fight another day."

"A wise decision," Rikki remarked.

"Are the Storm Police on your tail?" Hickok queried.

"No," Locklin replied. "They didn't follow us into the storm drain."

"That's strange," Hickok commented.

"We must leave the drain," Rikki declared.

Locklin stared to the rear. "Are you thinking what I'm thinking? That this must be a trap?"

"Why else wouldn't the Storm Police enter the drain?" Rikki rejoined.

"How can we get out of here?" Hickok interjected.

"There are manholes in the top every fifty yards," Locklin said. "We can climb out at the first one we find. I planned to use a manhole near the Civil Directorate, but the Storm Police might be waiting for us there."

"The troopers could be covering all the manholes," Rikki noted.

"I just can't understand how they knew," Locklin commented. "How did they know where to ambush us?"

Hickok noticed Dale abruptly stare downward.

"Stay close to me," Rikki recommended, and jogged along the conduit.

They traveled speedily, their footfalls and breathing unnaturally sonorous in the confines of the drain.

"There's a manhole!" Locklin exclaimed.

The flickering flame illuminated a brown metal cover overhead.

"Allow me," Locklin said, and stepped under the manhole. He reached up and pushed, but the manhole cover wouldn't budge.

"Let me give it a try, boss," Big John proposed.

"Go for it," Locklin responded, moving aside.

Big John applied his brawny left shoulder to the cover. For a minute he puffed and strained, to no avail.

"This is odd," Locklin commented. "It should open."

"Let's find another," Rikki suggested, leading off with the lighter held aloft.

Hickok fell in beside Dale. "How are you holdin' up, buckaroo?"

The youth looked warily at the Warrior. "Just fine, thanks."

"Were you nicked in the fracas?"

"No." He hefted the long bow in his right hand.

"Lucky you."

"What's that supposed to mean?" Dale asked.

"Nothin' much. I was just makin' conversation."

Dale studied the gunman, striving to see Hickok's face in the gloom.

"How long have you been with Locklin?" Hickok inquired.

"Three years."

"Have you seen a lot of action?"

"Enough."

"Ever seen anyone die before?" Hickok questioned.

"All the time," Dale replied. "I've done my share of

killing, you know. I helped ambush several Storm Police patrols.''

"Seein' an enemy die is one thing," Hickok observed. "Seein' friends die is another. Ever seen your friends die before?"

"Once or twice," Dale admitted.

"But not like tonight?" Hickok queried.

"No," Dale said angrily. "Now why don't we drop the subject?"

"If you want," Hickok said.

"I want to drop it," Dale reiterated.

"And well you should," Hickok stated. "All things considered."

Dale looked at the man in buckskins, perplexed. "Like what?"

"Like the fact you turned traitor," Hickok responded, his tone hardening. "Like the fact you were responsible for the ambush."

Dale halted and raised his left fist. "What the hell are you babbling about?"

Everyone halted.

"You betrayed your pards," Hickok told the youth.

Dale reached for a knife on his left hip. "I'll make you eat those words!"

The gunman's Uzi suddenly pointed at the youth's stomach. "I don't cotton to folks callin' me a liar."

"What is this?" Locklin demanded, glancing from Hickok to Dale in confusion. "Are you serious?" he asked the Warrior.

Hickok nodded. "Dale set you up."

"I did not!" Dale protested, flushing with fury.

"Do you have proof?" Locklin inquired.

"He'll tell you himself," Hickok said.

"You're crazy!" Dale declared.

"So everybody says," Hickok agreed. "And this crazy hombre is pointin' a machine gun at your innards. I'll count to three. If you haven't spilled the beans by then, you're dead."

The band of Freedom Fighters was watching in fascination, and none displayed the slightest inclination to interfere.

"Did you betray us?" Locklin asked the youth.

"How can you take his word over mine?" Dale snapped.

"One," Hickok said.

"I resent the accusation," Dale said. "We've lived and fought side by side. And this is the thanks I get?"

"Two."

Dale scanned the dim features of his companions for support, then looked at Locklin. "You're not going to let him shoot me in cold blood, are you? I'm one of your men." A hint of desperation made his voice quaver.

"Thr—" Hickok began.

"Don't shoot!" Dale cried, releasing his bow and elevating his arms. "Don't shoot!"

"Tell them the truth," Hickok ordered.

Dale's chin slumped to his chest. "I did it," he mumbled.

"What?" Locklin asked in disbelief.

"I gave our plans away," Dale said. "I told the Storm Police which drain we intended to use. I helped them set the trap."

There was a murmuring among the band.

Locklin stepped up to the youth and grabbed the front of Dale's shirt. "You did *what*?"

"I didn't have any choice!" Dale wailed, his lips trembling, his voice breaking. "They forced me!"

"Who?" Locklin asked the young rebel.

"The Storm Police," Dale said.

Locklin placed his hands on the youth's shoulder. "How could they coerce you into becoming a traitor? What could they possibly do?"

Dale stared into Locklin's accusing eyes, his own filling with tears. "They have my mother!" he said, and sobbed.

An awkward silence descended on the drain.

"Your mother?" Locklin repeated after a moment.

Dale hung his head, embarrassed by his tears. "Yes," he confirmed weakly.

"Tell us," Locklin urged softly.

The youth took a deep breath. "Do you remember last night, when my younger brother showed up at our camp?"

"Of course," Locklin said.

"My brother claimed our mother wanted to see me right away," Dale disclosed. "He told me that she was sick, real sick." He paused. "I went with him to our house."

"How did you get into the city?" Locklin interrupted.

"Through the usual route," Dale answered. "The sewer outlet under the southeast wall. My brother used the same way to leave. I followed your procedure to the letter."

Locklin gazed at the Warriors. "We've utilized certain sewer outlets frequently since the Storm Police barred the drains. Our families use them when they need to contact us," he explained. "The Storm Police didn't bar all the sewer outlets, probably because the outlets are so small only one person can slip through at a time and the sewers reek. They must figure only an absolute lunatic would use them."

"What happened when you got home?" Big John asked Dale.

"The Storm Police were waiting for me," Dale revealed. "They had discovered I was one of the Freedom Fighters, and they offered me a deal."

"Let me guess," Locklin said. "They promised to let your family live if you betrayed us?"

Dale sobbed. "God help me. Yes."

"You knew we intended to enter Atlanta tonight through this drain," Locklin mentioned.

"I sold you out," Dale declared forlornly.

"You had a tough choice to make," Hickok said, sympathizing.

"We all have one to make right now," Rikki-Tikki-Tavi mentioned. "Listen." He let the lighter go out.

Boot heels were pounding in the storm drain, approaching from the direction of the outer wall.

"The Storm Police!" Locklin exclaimed.

"And look!" Big John said, pointing directly ahead. Far off, their flashlight beams fingers of lights in the gloomy darkness, advancing at the double, were more troopers.

"We're cornered!" one of the Freedom Fighters cried.

Hickok looked both ways. "This is gettin' serious."

Chapter Nineteen

The room dissolved into bedlam.

Blade crammed the sheaths under his belt as he started to turn. He whipped the big knives out, the blades gleaming in the fluorescent light, and the first to feel his wrath was Eldred Morley. The Peer stood and foolishly lunged at the Warrior. Blade countered with a left elbow to the nose, feeling Morley's nostrils flatten with a pronounced crunch. The Peer was slammed backwards and toppled over his chair.

"Stop the bastard!" Lilith Friekan barked.

A trio of Storm Police tried. They were the nearest to the giant, their blackjacks out and ready, when he waded into them with his knives flashing.

Blade planted his left Bowie in the throat of a lean trooper. Even as he wrenched the left knife free, he stabbed the right blade into the chest of a second policeman, then spun and imbedded both Bowies in the third, one knife on each side of the hapless man's neck.

"*Get him!*" Sol Diekrick thundered, moving toward the giant.

Other than an enraged Lilith, the other Peers were too stunned to intervene.

The Storm Police were surging forward.

Blade jerked his Bowies clear, blood spurting from the third trooper's severed veins and arteries, and kicked, ramming his right boot into the man's chest and sending the body sailing into the charging police. As the lead troopers tumbled to the floor in a mass of thrashing arms and legs, he spun, sliding the Bowies into their sheaths, and bounded toward Sol Diekrick.

Sol attempted to land a right cross on the giant's chin.

With the speed and precision of a seasoned professional, Blade ducked under the wild swing and drove his right fist into Diekrick's abdomen, doubling the Peer over. He clamped his right hand on Sol's throat and seized his foe's groin in his left, then easily hoisted the struggling, gasping Peer overhead.

Stupefied by this display of monumental strength, the Storm Police, involved in untangling themselves from their pileup, momentarily froze, gawking.

"Kill the son of a bitch!" Lilith commanded.

Sol Diekrick's face was beet red, and he was gurgling and sputtering.

"Do you want your precious Peer?" Blade demanded, glaring defiantly at the troopers. "Then take him!" So saying, he whirled toward the Polyperv pane, took two lengthy strides, and hurled Sol at the window with all the power in his awesome physique.

Diekrick screamed as he impacted the pane. There was a rending crash as the Polyperv fractured and shattered, and both Peer and window plunged from sight.

"No!" Lilith screeched.

Blade took another step and leaped, sailing over the sill, tucking his legs under him as he plummeted, angling for a safe landing on the Polyperv-littered floor 20 feet below. He glimpsed Sol Diekrick lying to his left as he came down, his muscles braced for the shock. The force of the drop caused him to stagger and pitch onto his knees, and the soles of his feet stung horrendously, but otherwise he was unharmed. He lurched erect, pausing to glance at Diekrick.

The Peer must have dropped onto his head. His crown and forehead were crushed, flattened to a fleshy pulp, and oozing blood in a crimson stream.

"After him!" the Storm Police captain shouted from above.

Blade craned his neck to see the troopers gathered at the window. None of them seemed eager to make the jump. He grinned and dashed into the maze, hunching over, knowing they couldn't spot him unless he stood.

So far, so good.

Now came the hard part.

He had to find Glisson, evade or dispose of the Terminator squad, locate an exit from the maze, and escape from Atlanta.

Was that all?

Blade reached a junction and crouched, wondering which way to go, when he heard the pad of a stealthy tread. He eased back, placed his palms on the floor, and peeked around the corner.

A Teminerator was rounding a corner on the right, his Fryer sweeping from side to side, alert and cautious.

Damn. The executioner must have seen him jump from the window!

Blade withdrew his head and rose, drawing his right Bowie. The silver suits worn by the Terminators were fireproof, but was the fabric impenetrable?

There was only one way to find out.

He clutched the hilt of the Bowie and counted slowly to ten, trying to gauge the Terminator's position, hoping the range wouldn't be too great. As he girded himself to vault into the open, he received aid from an unexpected source.

The Storm Police had spotted him, and they saw the Terminator approaching the giant's position.

"Look out!" the captain yelled from the window.

"There! In front of you!" another shouted.

Blade sprang into the passage, his right arm sweeping back.

Distracted by the calls from above, the Terminator was gazing at the Storm Police, the Fryer nozzle held near his knees.

Blade never gave the Terminator the opportunity to bring

the Fryer into play. He tossed the Bowie from a distance of three yards, a maneuver he had practiced countless times at the Home on a variety of targets. Whether he threw the knife by the hilt or the blade, he invariably hit his mark. And now, once again, he demonstrated why his reputation had spread far and wide.

The Bowie streaked through the air and sliced into the Terminator between the eyes, lodging in the narrow strip of fabric separating the tinted eyepieces, sinking to the hilt. A muffled, indistinct cry sounded as the Terminator staggered backwards, waving the Fryer wildly, then collapsed.

Blade reached the body in three strides, stooped, and yanked the Bowie out.

One down, three to go.

But where were they?

He bent over at the waist and jogged into the labyrinth. To reach one of the doors, not to mention finding Glisson, could entail hours of winding through the bewildering maze—unless he came up with a brainstorm. He could try slashing signs in the fireproof fabric covering the walls, but doing so would involve using time he couldn't afford to spare. The Storm Police might not jump from the smashed window, but they would certainly regroup and descend to the maze chamber by whatever stairway connected the floors.

What to do?

Blade stopped and crouched, studying the walls all around him. They were only six feet in height, enabling him to gaze over them if he rose to his full stature. He could probably spot Glisson and the Terminators, but the doors would not be visible. Nor would the proper sequence of passages he needed to take to exit the maze be readily apparent.

No.

An extra foot wouldn't make a difference.

But what about seven extra feet?

The insight brought a smile to his lips. Although the maze

walls were six feet high, above them was a gap of thirty feet to the ceiling, undoubtedly designed to permit the Peers to view events from their room.

Would it work?

Blade straightened, replaced the right Bowie in its sheath, and climbed onto the rim of the wall. The silvery tops of the Terminators' helmets were easy to spy. One was 40 yards to his right. The second was two dozen yards straight ahead. And the third was to his left, perhaps 20 feet off and moving away from him.

Glisson wasn't in view.

What was the tramp doing? Hiding?

Blade cupped his hands to his mouth. "Glisson! Where are you?"

The three Terminators halted, their silver headpieces miniature islands of stark contrast in an ocean of brown walls.

There was no reply.

"Glisson!" Blade shouted. "It's Blade! Where are you, you numbskull?"

From off to the right came a feeble response. "Blade? Is that you?"

"Of course it's me!" Blade assured the hobo. "Stand up so I can see you!"

Their silvery heads twisting every which way, the Terminators, obviously disconcerted by all the yelling, were attempting to figure out what was going on.

"If I stand up, the Terminators will fry my ass," Glisson declared.

"If you want my help escaping from this maze, then you'd better stand up!" Blade said. "Right now!"

Glisson's thatch of dark hair popped up, midway between the Warrior and a Terminator. "Where are you?"

"Never mind," Blade answered. "Don't move. I'll be right there." He glanced around and spied one of the Terminators, the one to his left, hastening toward him. He decided to act on his idea. Why should he travel *through* the maze, never knowing when he might bump into a

Terminator, his sense of direction all askew, when he could take an alternate route?

On top of the walls!

Blade moved toward the tramp, his boots easily negotiating the six-inch-wide top of each wall, the fireproof material feeling slightly spongy underfoot. The passages seldom ran straight for any span, and he was compelled to follow a circuitous path to Glisson, constantly turning with the sharp angles of the walls.

"Where are you?" Glisson called out.

"Just don't move," Blade replied. He spotted a Terminator ahead and skirted wide of the assassin.

"Hey!" exclaimed a muted voice to his left. "The guy who came through the window is on one of the walls!"

Blade paused and scrutinized the maze.

A Terminator was staring at him from 30 feet away.

"Where are you?" Glisson said yet again.

The Warrior hurried, knowing the Terminators would be after him, and hoping they would be impeded by the labyrinth and unable to get within flamethrower range.

"You on the wall!" bellowed one of the Terminators.

"Who the hell is he?" demanded another.

"He must be part of the contest," assumed the third.

"Should we switch to infrared?" asked the first Terminator.

"What for?" retorted the first. "So long as he stays on the walls, we can see him. And if he drops down, the damn metal in the walls will interfere with our Heat Vision sensors."

Blade listened to their exchange with interest. Infrared? Their suits must incorporate a heat-tracking mechanism, a means of locking on the body heat generated by their quarry. He turned right, then took a sharp left, drawing ever nearer to Glisson.

The old-timer had finally seen the Warrior. He was gawking at Blade in frank astonishment.

"I've got him!" one of the Terminators cried.

Blade glanced to his right, and there was a Terminator

running in pursuit, not more than 15 feet off but separated by two walls.

The silvery form stopped and elevated the Fryer nozzle, aiming at the giant.

Blade leaped to the passage below before the Terminator could fire. He sprinted to the end of the corridor and turned left at the first junction, then right at the next.

Glisson was 20 feet away, and he smiled broadly as the Warrior came into view. "Blade!"

"We must reach one of the doors," Blade declared as he ran forward. Less than a dozen feet remained to be covered when the hobo's mouth slackened in alarm and he pointed at something to Blade's rear.

"Look out!" he shouted.

Reacting instinctively, Blade threw himself to the floor, scuffing his elbows and knees. Sudden, blistering heat prickled the back of his body from his head to his toes. He saw a tongue of red and orange flame shoot overhead.

The fire enveloped Glisson.

Screaming in terror, ineffectually swatting at the flames, the tramp staggered backwards as his clothes combusted. He shrieked, spinning in circles, smacking his clothing repeatedly. "Help me!" he wailed.

Prevented from rising by the sheet of flame, Blade watched, shocked, as Glisson burned to death. Not more than 30 seconds elasped between the moment Glisson was struck by the flames and his near-total incineration. His flesh blackened almost immediately, and he seemed to shrivel as the scorching heat engulfed him. The last sound he uttered was a pitiable whimper.

And still the Terminator poured on the flames.

Blade twisted on his stomach, squinting, trying to see the assassin but hampered by the flames. He realized the Terminator could not see him either, and he slid toward the killer, hoping he could reach the silvery slayer before the Terminator lowered the wall of shooting fire. His heart pounding, he crawled quickly until he detected a pair of silver boots a few feet in front of him.

There the bastard was!

His countenance set in grim lines, Blade pulled himself closer and reached out, gripping the Terminator's ankles in his viselike hands and surging up and in. Excruciating, scalding anguish lanced his back, and the putrid scent of burning flesh, *his* burning flesh, assailed his nostrils. He rose, upending the Terminator.

As the killer fell, he lost his grip on the Fryer nozzle and the flamethrower quit spitting fire.

Blade held onto the Terminator's ankles, and when the executioner fell onto the tanks with a loud clang, he savagely extended the Terminator's legs as far as he could reach.

The man in the silver attire screeched as his groin was seared by exquisite torment.

In a cold, fierce fury, Blade kicked the Terminator where it would hurt the most, then released the man's ankles and pounced on the killer's chest, his knees gouging into the Terminator's ribs. He drew the Bowies, the blades glistening as they arced through the air, and he sank the knives into the Terminator's eyepieces, one in each eye.

Bucking and convulsing, the Terminator's demise was grisly and fitting.

Blade tugged the Bowies loose and stood slowly, his gray eyes smoldering. He looked over his right shoulder at the charred form of his former acquaintance, then stalked into the maze, the knives at his sides. He wasn't running anymore.

There was a score to settle.

He threaded through the labyrinth, seeking the last pair of Terminators, and he came on them both simultaneously, rounding a corner.

Neither Terminator spotted the Warrior. Their backs were to him, and they were involved in an earnest discussion.

". . . lost sight of him," one was saying.

"And I haven't seen Cooper anywhere," said the second.

"Do you think that big son of a bitch got them?"

The second Terminator shrugged. "I don't know. Who *is* he? I heard a crash and looked up in time to see him drop down."

"I thought I saw a body fall first."

"We should stick together," suggested the second. "We'll have a better chance of nailing the big guy."

"If he's alive," remarked the first. "Did you hear those screams?"

"I'm alive," declared a firm voice behind them. "Why don't you come and get me?"

They swiveled, bringing up their Fryers.

Blade darted to the right, sprinted along a short passage, and turned to the left. He paused in the junction and waited, his expression steely.

A second later the Terminators jogged into view.

"Here I am!" Blade taunted them, and took off again. He weaved through the maze, never running at his full speed, deliberately holding back so the Terminators wouldn't lose him. Whenever they managed to narrow the distance, he would increase the pace enough to preserve his lead. He was playing a deadly game of cat and mouse, and he led the pair on a winding chase for over ten minutes.

"Slow down and fight, you prick!" one of them yelled, frustrated by their failure to catch the giant.

"We want your ass!" snapped the second.

Blade reached an intersection and looked back, and as they came into sight he raced to the left. They were angry, and probably fatigued, and such a combination inevitably resulted in carelessness.

Now was the time to finish it.

He veered into a right-hand corridor, placed the Bowies in his sheaths, and executed a flying leap. His fingers closed on the lip of the right-hand wall, and he hauled himself up with fluid ease and flattened.

"Where the hell did he go?" a Terminator bellowed from the passage the Warrior had just vacated.

Blade slid closer to the junction until his boots were at the corner. He placed his palms on the edges of the wall and tensed. If the men in the silver suits were as provoked as he expected, they would come barreling around the corner without bothering to look upward.

An instant later, they did.

Blade sprang, his body serving as a massive projectile as he launched himself into a flying tackle. They were side by side when he plowed into them from behind, his arms looping around their waists, his momentum bowling them over.

Encumbered by their tanks and their Fryer nozzles, the Terminators were awkward in recovering.

Blade was on his feet first, and he grabbed the left arm of the nearest Terminator and twisted sharply until there was a distinct snap.

The Terminator shrieked.

Remorseless in his revenge, Blade swept his left leg into the other Terminator, who was trying to stand, and knocked the man to the floor. Still grasping the arm of the injured assassin, he gripped the wrist in his right hand, the shoulder in his left, and drove his right knee into the man's elbow.

There was a popping sound and the Terminator voiced a shrill cry.

Blade flung the first man to the floor.

The second Terminator heaved erect. At such close quarters he could not employ his flamethrower for fear of incinerating his companion. Instead, he lashed out with his right boot.

A piercing pain racked Blade's left kneecap and he inadvertently doubled over.

Pressing his advantage, the second Terminator aimed a kick at the giant's face. The blow never landed.

Blade caught the Terminator's boot in his hands and wrenched the leg, rotating the boot clockwise until his adversary vented a muffled oath and toppled to the right. Mentally suppressing the torment caused by his throbbing knee, Blade closed in and planted the knobby knuckles of his right fist on the Terminator's headpiece, at the point where he estimated the man's chin to be, as the silvery executioner was scrambling upward.

The Terminator went flying and crashed onto his back.

His ponderous fists clenched, Blade stalked forward, moving methodically, not bothering to draw his Bowies. He saw the Terminator struggling to rise yet again, and he waited until the man was almost upright before striking.

Wobbly, his hands limp at his sides, the Fryer nozzle dangling by its hose from the tanks, the Terminator was on his last legs.

Blade didn't care. He slugged the man twice, a right and a left, and the Terminator, out on his feet, toppled over, falling forward instead of backwards. Blade caught the man in his arms, and he was about to toss the assassin aside when a cold voice dictated otherwise.

"Don't move, asshole!" barked someone to his rear.

Blade froze, supporting the Terminator by the armpits.

"I want to see the look on your puss when I squeeze the trigger," the person declared. "So when I tell you to turn around, do it very, very carefully. If you understand, nod."

The Warrior nodded.

"Good. Now turn around, real slow."

Holding onto the Terminator, Blade pivoted.

"You should have finished me off."

"I know," Blade said. "There wasn't time. I was getting to you next."

The Terminator with the broken left arm was six feet away, his broken limb bent at an unnatural angle, his hand hanging useless next to his waist. In his right hand was his Fryer nozzle, his finger on the trigger. "I'll enjoy watching you burn, you son of a bitch."

"What about your friend here?" Blade asked, hefting the unconscious form.

"Put Johnston down," the Terminator directed.

Blade deposited the silver figure on the floor.

"Now step back," the first Terminator ordered.

His mind racing, Blade took a stride backwards. Unless he thought fast, he would be burnt to a crisp. There was no way he could pull his Bowies before the Terminator fired. He needed a diversion. But what? Glisson was dead and couldn't be of any help.

Or could he?

Blade recalled the conversation he'd overheard between the two executioners. They mentioned having heard screams, but they didn't know *who was doing the screaming*. They didn't know Glisson was dead. He had a chance, then, to outwit the one in front of him, but to do so meant relying upon the oldest trick in the book.

"Are you ready to die, you suck-egg bastard?" the Terminator taunted him.

"Not yet," Blade responded, glancing quickly over the Terminator's left shoulder and widening his eyes, pretending to have seen someone. He immediately adopted a placid expression, as if he was hiding the fact.

The Terminator took the bait and glanced over his left shoulder, and out of the corner of his right eye he detected the giant coming at him. He started to face his enemy, cutting loose with the Fryer before his turn was completed, intending to consume the meddler with flames. He nearly succeeded.

Blade knew he couldn't reach the Terminator before the man fired, and he also was aware he couldn't clamber over the walls in time. Employing the Bowies was a dubious proposition; the Terminator might manage to squeeze off a burst of flame. His best bet was to interpose something—anything—between the Terminator and himself. And there was only one object available.

The unconscious Terminator.

Moving rapidly for a man of his size, Blade stooped, seized the insensate Terminator by the shoulders, and lifted, his muscles rippling. He was shoving his makeshift shield at the first Terminator when the Fryer nozzle spat red and orange, the flames striking the tanks on the back of the second Terminator. The result, to the Warrior, at least, was unexpected.

There was a tremendous explosion.

Blade felt a jarring concussion as he was lifted and

catapulted backwards, tumbling end over end, his hands
and arms tingling, his face blistered. Disoriented, he
crashed to the floor and slid over 20 feet, thumping to a
bone-rattling stop against a wall at the next junction. He
wound up on his left side, stunned, staring at the vestige
of a glowing fireball dissipating in the passage.

Dear Spirit!

He rose to his knees slowly, his ears ringing, realizing
the tanks on the second Terminator must have exploded
and the man's body had screened his own.

But what about the first Terminator?

Blade stood and walked slowly along the seared hall,
amazed to discover a small crater in the middle of the floor.
Smoky tendrils wafted toward the ceiling. And beyond the
crater was an indeterminate mass of charred . . . something.

"What the hell was that?" called a deep voice.

"Did you see that blast?"

"Fan out! Find him!"

Blade climbed quickly onto the left-hand wall. He raised
his head cautiously and surveyed the chamber.

Dozens of Storm Police were pouring through the door
on the right side of the maze chamber, spreading into the
maze, seeking him. But there was no indication of activity
at the door on the left.

Perfect.

Still feeling slightly unsteady, Blade rose to a crouch and
headed for the left wall. His sole purpose now was to escape
from Atlanta and rejoin Hickok and Rikki. Glisson was
gone. And there wasn't any reason to locate Llewellyn
Snow. If she had betrayed her sister-in-law, she would
hardly welcome Leslie Snow's child into her home.
Besides, the Peers wanted Chastity exterminated. The
Warriors would watch over the girl for the time being, until
a suitable home could be found. He focused on the door
in the center of the left wall, his teeth gritting in resolve.

No more pussyfooting around.

If anyone stood in his way, he'd slay them on the spot.

He crossed the maze without being spotted by the Storm Police and jumped to the floor near the door. In three bounds he was through the doorway and in a brightly lit stairwell. He peered upward, elated to discover the stairwell was empty. Grinning in anticipation of regaining his freedom, he ascended the stairs, taking four at a stride. A landing appeared with a door marked SUBLEVEL 5. He kept going. The next landing was SUBLEVEL 4. With renewed vigor, he passed landing after landing until he found the one he wanted.

GROUND LEVEL.

Blade tried the doorknob and it twisted in his grasp. With a smile creasing his features, he stepped boldly outside, into the night.

Only to find two figures rushing at him.

Chapter Twenty

"We won't go down without a fight," Locklin said, notching an arrow on his bow string.

"Do you ever use guns?" Hickok asked.

Locklin did a double take. "What difference does it make at a time like this?"

Hickok glanced at the two groups of approaching Storm Police. "Answer me. Do you ever use guns?"

"Once in every blue moon," Locklin answered. "Why?"

The gunman looked at Rikki. "Do you get my drift, pard?"

Rikki-Tikki-Tavi nodded.

"Are you with me?" Hickok queried.

"Need you ask?"

"Will one of you tell me what's going on?" Locklin demanded.

"The Storm Police expect rebels to use bows," Hickok said. "We might rattle them a mite with our irons."

"All you have are a pair of Uzis and two revolvers," Locklin noted.

Hickok nodded at the troopers in front of them, now about 50 yards distant. "They don't know how many guns we have." He paused. "I never should've left the M-16 with your man Scarlet."

"You wanted him to be able to protect Chastity

properly,'' Rikki reminded the gunfighter.

"Cryin' over spilt milk never helped anyone," Hickok stated. "Are you ready?"

"Ready," Rikki confirmed.

"What's your plan?" Locklin inquired.

"Simple. We'll charge the varmints."

Locklin couldn't seem to believe his ears. "*We're* going to charge *them*?"

"Yep."

"There are sixteen of us and dozens of them," Locklin pointed out.

"Good. We won't need to aim as hard."

Locklin shook his head. "You're crazy."

The gunman looked at Rikki. "Why the blazes does everyone keep saying that?"

The martial artist shrugged. "Beats me."

"If we're going to charge, why don't we charge *them*?" Locklin asked, and pointed at the Storm Police drawing nearer from their rear, from the direction of the outside wall. "If we break through, we'll be in the forest before they can catch us."

"You can charge them if you want," Hickok said. "But we're chargin' the turkeys in front. We're not leavin' without Blade."

"You can come back for Blade another time," Locklin suggested.

"A Warrior never deserts another Warrior," Hickok stated. "Never."

Locklin gazed at his band. "You heard him. Stay close to me."

"What about me?" Dale inquired.

"What *about* you?" Locklin answered. "You're a member of the Freedom Fighters. Behave like one."

Dale blinked a few times and swallowed hard.

"On me," Hickok directed. He glanced at Rikki. "If something should happen to me, make sure Chastity finds a nice home."

"She will," Rikki promised.

Hickok grinned and faced the Storm Police 40 yards away. "Don't fire until you can see their britches," he said, and raced forward.

"Britches?" Locklin repeated quizzically as he followed.

The gunman concentrated on the flashlight beams sweeping the drain. Those beams illuminated a 25-to-30 yard stretch of conduit ahead of the advancing troopers. He would need to time this just right.

Rikki was staying abreast of the gunfighter.

Hickok cradled the Uzi. "This is for Chastity's mom and dad," he said under his breath. He sprinted into the outer fringe of light cast by the beams and opened fire.

Beside the gunman, Rikki promptly added his Uzi to the din.

"Remember the Alamo!" Hickok shouted, his moccasins pounding on the concrete.

The flashlights began waving frantically, and several shattered and blinked out. Screams and yells punctuated the gunfire. A milling of shadows cast eerie reflections on the drain as the Storm Police wavered. A half dozen dropped in the initial seconds of the attack, and those unharmed seemed to believe that a horde of rebels was pouring toward them. A few desultory rounds were expended, and then the rest broke and bolted.

"Halt! Stand your ground!" a captain bellowed, and was flattened by a hail of slugs.

"Take no prisoners!" Hickok whooped.

"For freedom!" Locklin chimed in.

The Storm Police did not show any appetite for combat. Except for a few hardy souls who snapped off occasional shots, the majority of the troopers appeared to be more interested in saving their skins then in dying in the line of duty.

Hickok slowed as he slapped a fresh magazine into the Uzi. "What a bunch of wimps!" he commented.

Rikki abruptly stopped.

"What is it?" Hickok asked, halting. The Freedom Fighters also drew up short.

"This is too easy," Rikki remarked. "Why are they fleeing?"

"Most of the Storm Police are not accustomed to resistance," Locklin said.

"But patrols are sent out to engage your band all the time," Rikki noted.

"They send their older troopers out to get us," Locklin responded. "The younger recruits are kept in the city. Only the older ones are assigned to rebel hunts, as the Peers call them. Evidently, the older troopers are considered more expendable. The younger ones, as a result, don't have much experience."

"Do we keep chasing them?" Big John inquired.

Hickok gazed at the fleeing Storm Police, their forms outlined by their receding flashlight beams. "No. They could be runnin' because they're greenhorns, and they could be leadin' us into another trap."

"What do we do then?" Locklin wanted to know.

"We get the blazes out of here," Hickok said.

"How?" Locklin inquired.

Rikki's lighter flicked on. "We must find an open manhole." He started walking deeper into the tunnel.

Hickok cocked his head to one side. "What about the troopers behind us? Are they still on our heels."

"I don't hear them," the last rebel in line replied.

"They must be tryin' to figure out what the dickens is happening," Hickok said. "Good. We've bought us a few minutes. Now—"

"Hickok," Rikki called from eight yards off.

The gunman hastened to his friend's side. "Have you found one, pard?"

For an answer, Rikki held the lighter aloft, revealing another manhole cover.

"Big John," Locklin directed.

Once again the biggest Freedom Fighter applied his brawny shoulder to the task, but with different results. As Big John grunted and arched his broad back, the manhole cover slowly eased to the left with a grinding noise. In less than a minute the cover was removed.

"I can see trees," Big John remarked, peering over the rim.

"Let me take a gander," Hickok said.

Big John moved to one side.

Holding the Uzi at chest height, just in case, Hickok stood on his toes and looked around. The conduit was situated in a sloping gully with cement sides and bordered by a chain-link fence. He glanced at Locklin. "Why is there a fence?"

"To keep the public out, especially the kids," Locklin replied. "When the drains were installed, the construction crews dug a trench, poured the concrete, and enclosed the whole deal as a safety measure."

Hickok placed the Uzi on the outer rim, then pulled himself to his knees. Beyond the fence on the right was a residential area, and on the left was a park. Streetlights at periodic intervals supplied a diffuse illumination, the closest light being 30 feet to the right. Thanks to an intervening tree, the manhole section was obscured by shadows. "The coast is clear," Hickok announced softly. "Everybody out." He walked a few yards from the manhole and scanned their surroundings.

Rikki, Locklin, and the rest of the band clambered speedily from the drain.

"Which way to the Civil Directorate?" Hickok asked the rebel leader.

Locklin pointed to the southwest. "It's not far."

"I just hope Blade is there," Hickok said.

"If you friend has been captured, the odds are he's there," Locklin stated. "But our first priority is taking care of the Peers."

"*Your* first priority is takin' care of the Peers," Hickok said, correcting him. "Ours is findin' our pard."

Locklin nodded at the park. "We can cut through here. That's Piedmont Park."

"Head 'em out," Hickok instructed.

Working in concert, with Big John providing a boost to

everyone who needed it, the Warriors and Freedom Fighters scaled the chain-link fence. Big John came over without assistance.

"Lead the way," Hickok said to Locklin.

Motioning for his band to fan out, Locklin headed into the lush park. They crossed a grassy knoll and reached a walkway, and there encountered their first citizens, a young couple strolling arm in arm. The man and woman took one look at the Freedom Fighters, with their unusual green attire, and took off to the southeast.

"Now we're in for it," Locklin said. "They'll report us to the police."

"I could catch them," Big John offered.

"We don't harm civilians," Locklin responded. "You know that."

"I could tie them up," Big John proposed.

"We keep going," Locklin declared.

They increased their pace, with Dale supporting a rebel with a wounded leg.

Several minutes went by.

"We have company," Rikki informed them.

Approaching from the southeast were more flashlights.

"Storm Police," Locklin said.

"We stand and fight," Hickok stated. "We don't want them doggin' us every step of the way."

Locklin headed toward a row of trees nearby. "Take cover!" he commanded. "Don't loose a shaft until I do."

Hickok and Rikki ran for cover behind a large maple tree. The gunman leaned on the trunk and watched the shining beams, estimating the troopers were within 50 yards. "I'm gettin' real tired of these cow chips."

"They know they have the rebels cornered in the city," Rikki observed, "and they will stop at nothing to eliminate the Freedom Fighters."

"Not if I can help it," Hickok vowed.

"What will we do if Blade is not in the Civil Directorate?" Rikki asked.

"We'll grab one of the Peers and throttle Blade's

whereabouts out of him. Or her, if they have such female polecats."

"You never have been one for subtlety."

"Beatin' around the bush is for the birds," Hickok said. "Roll with the flow, I always say."

"Can you translate that?"

"When I was eight, I learned one of the most important lessons of my life," Hickok explained. "There was this bully by the name of Greer—"

"I remember him," Rikki said, interrupting. "He was always picking fights with the younger children in our Family."

"And he picked one with me," Hickok detailed. "I got in a few licks, but he walloped me good. My mom couldn't help but notice my swollen cheek and black eyes, so I had to tell her everything. She told me to go to Greer and offer my hand in friendship. She said that Greer would respond if I was sincere. 'Blessed are the peacemakers' was the creed she lived by."

"What happened?" Rikki whispered.

"I walked up to Greer, smilin' and sincere, and informed him I wanted to be his good buddy."

"What did Greer do?"

"What else? He busted me in the chops." Hickok paused. "I tore into him, and the second time around I came out on top. Greer left me alone after that. I . . . ." He stopped, gazing at the troopers.

The Storm Police were filing under an overhead park light. There were two dozen plus an officer, and all of them were armed with automatic weapons. Ten troopers in front were probing the vegetation with flashlights. Although 20-foot-high overhead lampposts were situated along the walkways, darkness enveloped most of Piedmont Park.

Hickok crouched and stared at the nearby trees. He had to hand it to the Freedom Fighters; he knew they were hiding there, but he couldn't see hide nor hair of one of them. At that moment, to his amazement, Big John walked brazenly into the open and hailed the troopers.

"Hey, you murdering slime! Here's what I think of you!" bellowed the big man, who then flipped them the finger, turned, and ran off.

Predictably, the Storm Police captain yelled, "Get him!" and the troopers raced in pursuit.

Hickok grinned at the success of the ruse. He saw the Storm Police pounding across the grass. The fleetest troopers were almost to the row of trees when the rebels stepped from cover and released their arrows. Thirteen shafts sped true to their mark, and with their first volley the Freedom Fighters downed half of the police.

The remainder recovered quickly.

A precious second was wasted as the rebels pulled arrows from their quivers and notched the shafts to their bows, and six of the Freedom Fighters were stitched by trooper fire before they could pull their bow strings.

"Let's join the fun," Hickok said, and leaped from behind the tree. He perforated the nearest policeman with a burst from the Uzi. Pivoting, he shot another.

The rebels and the troopers were now intermixed and fighting hand to hand. Some of the Freedom Fighters were using knives, while bayonets were being wielded skillfully by many of the Storm Police. At such close range the troopers could not bring their automatic rifles into play, and the brutal battle was waged in terms of survival of the deadliest.

A tall trooper suddenly appeared out of the melee and charged the gunman.

Hickok glimpsed the policeman out of the corner of his eye and tried to turn, but a smashing blow from the trooper's rifle stock on his chin knocked him to the ground, dazed. The Uzi fell from his fingers, and he looked up to see the Storm Policeman drawing a bayonet. He shook his head and tried to rise.

"I'm going to gut you like a fish," the trooper gloated, stabbing the bayonet at the Warrior's midsection.

But the bayonet never connected.

A gleaming streak of steel intercepted the trooper's

bayonet arm, slicing through the Storm Policeman's wrist as easily as a hot knife through butter. The trooper's eyes bulged and he straightened, screaming, as the steel blade arced into his neck, partially severing his throat. Blood spurted everywhere, and the trooper toppled backwards.

Hickok's senses returned in a rush, and there was Rikki-Tikki-Tavi standing over him.

"Will you quit goofing off?" the martial artist quipped, his crimson-covered katana in his right hand. Before the gunman could respond, he whirled and waded into the conflict. A stroke of the katana ruptured a trooper's abdomen, and a second swipe hacked off a policeman's left arm.

Hickok shoved to his feet, and as he rose he heard a loud whomp-whomp-whomp from above. Puzzled, he craned his neck skyward, surprise registering on his features.

A large green helicopter was hovering over the swirling combatants, training a spotlight on the grim fight. On one side was an open sliding door, and perched in the doorway was a marksman in a Storm Police uniform, a rifle with an infrared scope pressed to his right shoulder.

Hickok saw the marksman fire, and one of the rebels fell as a high-caliber slug penetrated his skull.

The marksman sighted on another target, the helicopter poised 50 feet above the grass.

Embroiled in their savage contest, the Freedom Fighters were unaware of this new threat. Three more of the rebels were lying on the turf, their lifeblood seeping into the soil.

Hickok took two strides to the left to give himself a better shot and drew his right Python, his thumb cocking the hammer even as the Colt came clear of its holster. The Magnum boomed once, and the marksman reacted as if he had been slammed in the head by a sledgehammer. Stiffening, the rifle dropping from his limp arms, the trooper pitched from the chopper.

With a whirring of its rotor, the helicopter banked and flew to the south.

What next? Hickok wondered, facing the fray. He saw

Rikki slice open a trooper's chest, the martial artist moving with superb precision and control. And as he scanned the battlefield, he spied a quartet of silvery forms coming from the west. The four were 30 yards distant and nearing the row of trees.

Why were they all silver?

Hickok suddenly recollected the Bubbleheads, and he dashed to a tree and pressed his back to the bole. He holstered the right Python, counted to ten, and on ten strolled into view, his thumbs hooked in his gunbelt.

Twenty yards off the Bubbleheads stopped, leveling their flamethrower nozzles.

"Howdy, gents," Hickok said, his hands seemingly invisible as both Pythons swept up and out. Each gun cracked twice, and with each retort a silvery figure was thrown backwards by the impact of a .357 slug striking his forehead. "Piece of cake," the gunfighter commented, and turned.

The combat had ended.

Bodies sprawled in attitudes of violent death littered the landscape. Groans and feeble cries filled the air. Puddles of blood splotched the grass. Only four of the rebels still stood. Locklin was gazing at his fallen companions somberly. Big John, a jagged wound in his left shoulder, was wiping his knife on his left pants leg. The two other rebels were exhausted but uninjured.

Hickok glanced to his right and spotted Rikki. The martial artist stood in the middle of a ring of three trooper corpses, his katana clenched in both hands, blood dripping from the blade. "Are you okay, pard?" Hickok asked.

Rikki nodded.

The gunman hurried to Locklin. "What about you?"

"I'm fine," Locklin said, picking up a discarded AR-15.

Hickok surveyed the bodies, and two yards away he beheld the rebel called Dale with a bayonet jutting from his thorax. "Your band has been decimated," he remarked.

"We can always get new recruits," Locklin said, sadness filling his eyes as he noticed the objects of Hickok's attention.

"We'd best vamoose," the gunman declared. "We must find Blade before more Storm Police show up."

"No," Locklin stated.

"No?"

Locklin nodded to the southeast. "We're too late."

Hickok looked in the same direction, frowning at the sight of additional Storm Police one hundred yards distant. "Blast!"

"The Civil Directorate is one of seven ten-story structures to the southwest. It's the third one from the north. You can't miss it," Locklin said.

"Why are you telling me this?" Hickok inquired.

"Because we'll never reach it if we all stick together," Locklin replied. "Rikki and you can get there by yourselves."

"And what about you?"

"My men and I will lead the Storm Police on a wildgoose chase," Locklin proposed. "If we can lure them to the north, you shouldn't have any trouble in reaching the Civil Directorate."

"I don't like the notion," Hickok said. "There's just the four of you left. The odds are too great."

"Do you want to save your friend?"

"Of course."

"Then don't argue. There isn't time," Locklin stated. Then he placed his right hand on the Warrior's shoulder. "I appreciate the thought. I really do. But I'm right and you know it." He paused. "Besides, don't count us out yet. We're experts at guerilla warfare, and the night is on our side. We can elude the Storm Police. And getting over the wall from inside is simple."

Rikki appeared at Hickok's left side. "He's right. We have no choice."

"I still don't like it," Hickok muttered. He extended his right hand. "May the Spirit be with you."

Locklin shook and smiled. "Thanks. If all goes well, we'll meet you where we left Scarlet and Jane."

"And Chastity," Hickok added.

"Good luck," Locklin said. He gestured at Big John and the two others, and they promptly jogged to the north.

Hickok and Rikki hastened on a southwesterly bearing, keeping well away from all lighted areas. After covering 75 yards they paused and glanced back. The second contingent of Storm Police had arrived at the site of the fight and was milling about. A smattering of gunfire from the north galvanized them into a rush to investigate the source of the shots.

"Locklin is as good as his word," Rikki remarked.

"He'd make a dandy Warrior," Hickok said. He looked at his friend. "Say, where's your Uzi?"

"I used the last of my ammo," Rikki responded. "Where's yours?"

"I plumb forgot all about it," Hickok answered, and shrugged. "Oh, well. I have my Colts, and they're all I need." He reloaded both revolvers quickly. "All set."

They resumed running, avoiding all civilians in their path until they came to a street on the south side of Piedmont Park. The street was jammed with pedestrians.

"What do we do?" Rikki asked, peering over the top of a shrub.

"We pretend we're tourists," Hickok suggested. "Stick your katana scabbard down your pants and walk with a limp. I can tuck my Pythons under my buckskin shirt. If we act like we now what we're doing, and if all of the Storm Police are out huntin' for rebels, we shouldn't have a problem."

"What if we do encounter Storm Police?"

"We do what we do best."

"No one will stop us," Rikki pledged.

The two Warriors blended into the pedestrian flow, following the sidewalks to the southwest. Locating the Civil Directorate was ridiculously easy; the monoliths were unique. It wasn't until they were standing at the edge of a parking lot located behind the Civil Directorate that Rikki made a critical observation.

"We'll stand out like sore thumbs in there."

"Then let's conk a couple of citizens on the noggin and swipe their clothes," Hickok recommended. He pointed at a door in the middle of the rear wall. "Look. There's some bushes near that door. We'll hide there and grab the first two civilians who come out."

"Lead on, brilliant one."

"Remind me to have you put that in writing," Hickok quipped, and headed across the parking lot. He was within 15 feet of the door when he realized the doorknob was turning, and he drew his right Colt as he closed the gap, hoping a citizen about his size would step through the doorway.

Instead, a giant emerged.

Epilogue

"What will you do?" Locklin asked.

"We'll continue searching for a means to return to the Home," Blade answered.

"At the rate we're going, we'll wind up walking there," Hickok said.

They stood on a hill 20 miles northwest of the metropolis. A blue, cloudless sky stretched to the far horizon.

"I can't wait to get to the Home," Chastity mentioned. "Walk fast."

"If you become tired," Rikki said with a grin, "Hickok will carry you."

"We'll all take turns carryin' her," Hickok stated.

Chastity took hold of the gunfighter's right hand. "Uncle Rikki and Uncle Blade are really nice. Are all the people at the Home like them?"

"All except one," Hickok replied.

"Who?"

"A mangy, low-down Injun by the name of Geronimo."

"What does he do?"

"He makes fun of me all the time."

The child's forehead creased. "But everyone does that."

Blade slapped his right thigh and laughed. "She'll make a wonderful addition to your family. I hope I'm there to see the expression on Sherry's face when you walk in the door."

"Forget it. This is a personal matter," Hickok said.

"Will your wife like me?" Chastity asked.

"Of course she will, princess," Hickok assured her.

Blade shook hands with Locklin. "It was a pleasure meeting you. I will report your case to the Freedom Federation Council."

"I hope they agree to aid us," Locklin said.

"We'll return and let you know," Blade promised.

The Warriors and the Freedom Fighters exchanged farewells. Chastity skipped to Rikki's side as the Warriors started down the hill.

Blade leaned toward the gunman. "How *will* you break the news to Sherry?" he whispered.

"I don't know," Hickok admitted. "But I have fourteen or fifteen hundred miles in which to come up with a bright idea."

"If she kicks you out of your cabin, you can always stay with us," Blade offered.

"Thanks, pard. But my missus would never boot me out. She's the sweetest, kindest person I know," Hickok said. Then he shook his head. "She'll probably stomp me silly, won't she?"

"Yep."

The gunfighter sighed. "I just hope she's in a good mood when we get there."

Chastity looked back and beamed. "Hurry up, Daddy!"

"A real good mood."